DeadHorse

Copyright © 2014 Travis Wright
Printed in the United States of America
Edited by Jenny Neyman
Illustrated by Melanie Noblin
Photographs by Logan Parks

This book is a work of fiction. The names, characters, places and incidents are products of the writer's imagination or have been used fictitiously and are not to be construed as real. Any resemblance to persons, living or dead, actual events, locales or organizations is entirely coincidental. While some of the locations used describe actual locations, this is intended only to lend an authentic theme for the book.

ISBN: 1940597994
ISBN 13: 9781940597997

DeadHorse

Travis Wright

This book is dedicated to all of my friends and family that have always believed in me and never left my side. You know who you are!

Life is entirely too short, and we all deserve to reach for the stars and be happy.

Chapter One

Kandahar, Afghanistan
Kandahar Airfield
Mark Mitchell, DOD contractor

It was another hot, dry morning in Kandahar. Mark Mitchell was still dragging ass after the last three-day mission. He left the bathhouse next to the troop barracks carrying his small shower bag with his toothbrush, toothpaste and shaving kit. He stood at a bit over six feet tall weighing around 200 pounds. Shaved bald, sporting a short-boxed beard, in good shape for a man in his late thirties. His Hawaiian tropical shirt was unbuttoned, his green khaki cargo pants faded and his combat boots currently unlaced. His gray Barrett cap was sun bleached, but the embroidered image of a Barrett 82A1 .50-caliber rifle was still visible. It was a favorite hat and a good luck charm that he'd had for years. He always made it out in one piece even on hot extractions. Could be the hat, could be a coincidence. Either way he continued to wear it because it fit just right.

He sighed as he walked past a thermometer reading almost ninety-seven degrees at nine in the morning. His dog tags swung back and forth around his neck. He had been off active duty for some time, but they had become a part of him, therefore they remained in place.

As the mirage created from the blistering heat rose from the concrete, Mark looked up as he heard a jet descending to land. A gold-and-white Gulfstream G650 lowered its wheels and glided onto the runway. Blue smoke rose from beneath it and the familiar rubber squeal could be heard.

Mark continued to walk until his trailer came into view, a yellow teardrop T@B that he called, "The Crypt". The outstretched awning covered a patch of Astroturf with a few camp chairs and a putting lane. Tiki torches and plastic pink flamingos sticking out of sandbags were positioned around the perimeter. As he approached the trailer, something caught his eye.

A blue Post-it note taped to the door read, *"Mark, come see me. We have a job for you. Victoria."*

Victoria was his main contact in the task force to which he was attached. Mark had known her for years, working with her on many occasions. The two of them had been an item at one time, but the job had always seemed to find its way between them. Even though there was still chemistry, they both knew that in their profession, it couldn't work. Regardless of how they felt, they always maintained a professional rapport, especially around other team members.

Mark crumpled the paper, put it in his pocket, opened the door and put his shower gear away. He grabbed his Glock 21C .45 ACP in its holster from the table, and picked up the 5.11 Tactical RUSH 12 back-pack by the door. He double-checked his gear and tied his boot-laces. Back outside he headed toward her office at the terminal.

He set off at a brisk clip, putting the backpack on and attaching the gun and holster to his belt and leg on the right side.

Once inside, it was clear this wasn't like a regular airport terminal. Soldiers from several nations swarmed the halls, sandbag barriers and checkpoints had been set up in certain areas. Most people inside carried live weapons, meaning they had a round in the chamber, with the safety on. This concept was explained to new people, especially civilians.

Mark made his way upstairs on the elevator and walked to a door marked as the entrance to a VIP lounge. At the door stood two men in digital camouflage fatigues with Military Police markings on the left upper sleeve. They glanced at his ID badge, with his picture and Department of Defense stamped across it in large letters, then waved him through. He walked in, carefully surveying the area as he had been trained to do. Nothing had changed since the last time he'd been there. He would have noticed.

The lounge had been converted into a make-shift office and command center to organize DOD contractors and military personnel alike. Victoria sat at her desk toward the far end of the room. As he walked in, she sat up in her leather high-back chair letting her long black hair hang free. She stretched her arms upwards, making her shirt cinch even tighter to her body, exposing her perfect curves. Mark looked, but he no longer dared touch. That was in the past, and it was all business now. She stood and adjusted her glasses, emerald green eyes peering through them. She walked over to Mark as he approached, handed him a file folder and began to explain the task at hand. The folder contained a few miscellaneous papers and a picture of a Middle Eastern man in his late forties. His name, Al Asari, appeared at the bottom.

Victoria began her briefing while twisting the high school class ring she wore on her wedding finger, a feint to throw men off. Mark's ears listened intently, but his eyes stared at her full lips instead of the photos on the table.

"That man is a field agent who's been collecting intel for us and the South Africans. He's currently waiting for retrieval at a fuel station just north of Erazi. He'll be behind the station pretending to work on a broken vehicle. You'll pick up a truck at the motor pool, drive out there and make contact. Then drive him back here and check in with me straight away. You might want to consider a change of clothes though," she asserted glancing up at him.

"You don't like my casual Friday shirt?" he said, with a slanted grin.

"It's nice, but it's a bit loud," Victoria replied, trying to hide a smile.

Mark memorized the contents of the folder and left it on her desk before heading down to the motor pool. A nice drive suited him on this hot morning. The objective would be an easy one, and he always accomplished his mission.

He stopped by his locker in the gear room on the lower level, retrieving the thawb and keffiyeh that were hanging inside. Wearing traditional dress would help him blend in with the locals. He slipped them over his current attire, unclasped the TAG Heuer Grand Carrera watch from his wrist and slid it into one of his cargo pockets.

At the motor pool he got into a Toyota Land Cruiser, flipped down the sun visor and the key fell into his lap. He put it in the ignition and fired up the turbocharged diesel V8. He rolled up to the gate, flashed his ID to the guard, signed out the vehicle, and drove away from the main terminal out of the secured area.

"Let's see what they left in the CD tray," Mark mumbled to himself. He turned on the multi-disk player and "Orion" by Metallica began bursting out of the speakers, so he turned it up accordingly.

Leaving the airport he had to weave through large concrete barriers, looking like over-sized versions of the jacks a kid would play with. He passed several checkpoints guarded by armored personnel carriers (APCs) and High-Mobility Multipurpose Wheeled Vehicles (HMMV's) with various machine guns on top.

Once he left the Green Zone he took the A75 North toward Kandahar's city center. The drive was uneventful, as usual, since a majority of the traffic was United States military forces. Mark looked just like any other local driving the road with what he was wearing, so neither the friendly military forces nor indigenous people paid him any attention.

Several kilometers after passing Haji Aziz, the A75 merged into the A1. As Mark approached Kandahar the traffic grew much denser and consisted of more civilian traffic than military.

He was a few blocks from taking the turn that would send him south towards Erazi when a vehicle-borne improvised explosive device (VBIED) detonated near where he planned on turning.

"Whoa there," he said, feeling the shock wave of the explosion. It took his breath away, even though the windows were up and the AC was on. Shrapnel and gravel pelted the Toyota, but didn't spider-web the windshield, since the vehicle was armored. Some of the military convoy vehicles that had been targeted were not so lucky.

Mark instantly cut down an alley, drove two streets over and got back on course, heading south on Shkarpor-Bazar-Kandahar. It had happened so quick that he couldn't discern exactly what vehicles had been hit. A massive cloud of dust and debris had been kicked up and enveloped the area, making it impossible to see.

Ten kilometers later he saw the fuel station that matched the given coordinates from the file. After a quick glance of the vicinity, he pulled into the drive and around to the rear. An older, beat-up Toyota HiLux sat near the back of the lot with its hood open. An Arabic-looking man, wearing what most locals wore - a tan shalwar kameez and a lungee on his head - was hunched over under the hood and appeared to be working on the engine. Mark drew closer and idled the vehicle for a moment before putting it in park and stepping out. He approached the man slowly and asked in flawless Arabic, "Do you need any help?" Mark slowly moved his hand closer to the Glock he had in his drop leg holster under his thawb.

The man working on the car put the wrench down slowly, stood up straight and stared intently at Mark as he said, "I think the fan is broken, it's overheating."

Following protocol, Mark then said the challenge, "My grandfather said it's supposed to storm this afternoon," as the Arabic man stood motionless.

"The weather has been hot recently," he replied.

Mark moved forward and gave the man a pat down for explosives or weapons. Once satisfied, he backed up again.

They both stared at each other for a split second before Mark said in English, "Get in."

Al Asari closed the hood of the truck and got in the passenger seat of the Land Cruiser. "Do you like heavy metal?" Mark asked.

Al Asari returned a blank stare.

"Like Megadeth, Slayer or Metallica?"

Al Asari looked even more confused and shook his head while saying, "I'm not sure what you speak of."

Mark turned the CD player on and pushed the track forward button a few times, until "Of Wolf and Man" by Metallica pulsed from the speakers.

The old man just shook his head again and looked out the window while Mark smiled at the conversation exchange, or lack thereof.

They pulled out, turning south on the road back toward Kandahar. Traffic had somewhat thinned out, which suited Mark just fine. By the time they drove near where the VBIED had detonated earlier, smoke could be seen rising above the buildings. The sound of AK-47 fire could be heard, mixed with M4 and .50-caliber fire in return. Mark drove closer and saw U.S. troops engaged with insurgents near where the blast had occurred. He could now see that only one Hummer had been destroyed, and by the looks of it, no one walked away. The tires had burned to the ground and the right side had been completely ripped from the shell.

There were civilians caught in the middle of the firefight. According to Al Jazeera and CNN there was always somebody innocent dying.

"Are any of us innocent?" Mark muttered to himself.

Al Asari gave him a strange look - this man sent to bring him in was talking to himself.

Mark pushed the accelerator and a cloud of black smoke was released from the exhaust pipe. He pushed in the clutch, ran up a gear and popped it out as they detoured around the skirmish.

They arrived back at Kandahar Airfield, without incident. Mark stopped at the gate where an M1 Abrams tank now sat with its main gun pointing at incoming traffic. He handed his ID and Al Asari's credentials to the guard.

"What's with the tank, Marine?" Mark inquired.

"After the attacks today, the base commander ordered it to guard the checkpoint."

"Makes sense, just curious of the new addition. Thanks, Devil Dog."

After waving him through, the Marine gave him an *"Oorah"* before Mark drove forward.

Immediately upon returning the vehicle to the motor pool, Mark and Al Asari made their way to Victoria's office.

"Al Asari, please come with me. Oh, and Mark, good job on the retrieval," she acknowledged. Her green eyes briefly glanced at him, and then looked away before she and Al Asari walked down the hallway, undoubtedly toward a briefing room.

Mark dropped his local dress in his locker and headed back to his trailer on the other side of the building, to lounge in his wading pool and catch some rays for the rest of the day. The highlight of his day was relaxing, after even the dullest of missions.

As he sat in a lounge chair that evening by the trailer, he noticed more aircraft than normal taking off, and troop movement around the base seemed suspicious.

Halfway through the night, Mark awoke to the sound of heavy knocking on the door of the trailer.

Who the hell is banging on my door? he thought, as he got up and stumbled through the trailer with his Glock in his hand. Looking through the blinds, he saw it was Victoria. He opened the door still half-asleep, wearing only a pair of blue boxers with red hearts on them.

"W-what do you want?" he asked, yawning. "I'm fucking sleeping."

"Not anymore," she announced, smirking while looking him up and down. "Get geared up and ready to roll in forty-five minutes. Al Asari gave us intel on a house holding what he called a very high-ranking Al-Qaeda target, possibly a general. Now wake up and meet us in the usual place. Operation Mongoose is about to kick off. And Mark, don't be late."

"Never am darling," he replied.

Victoria flipped her long hair to the side and walked away without another word, but Mark knew her all too well and could tell she was just hiding her smile.

He understood the drill, even though it had interrupted his sleep. He went to the sink and splashed cold water on his face to wake himself up.

Throwing on his khaki cargo pants, a black T-shirt and a dark green hoody, he grabbed his favorite noise-canceling aviation headset. He attached a Streamlight flashlight to the under-barrel rail of his Glock and slipped it into the Safariland drop leg holster. He secured it onto his belt and leg and headed off to a small meeting area set up in the banquet room inside one of the shut-down restaurants at the terminal.

Chapter Two

Kandahar, Afghanistan
'The Cave'
Mark Mitchell, DOD contractor

A SEAL team sat around the table while Mark stood at the rear of the room with his arms crossed. Victoria entered and pressed a button on a small remote. A projector clicked on. On the screen was a rough-looking man with a scraggly beard. His name appeared below the picture: Umar Abdul.

Mark knew Umar meant "man of his word," and Abdul roughly translated to "leader."

"Who is this guy?" drawled a stocky master chief with his uniform stretched tight over his torso and thick, 5 o'clock shadow covering his face.

"He is a high-ranking general for the extremist group Al-Qaeda," replied Victoria.

"Why haven't we ever heard of him?" a young petty officer with an obviously tailored shirt, chimed in.

"We had believed him to be a low-level player, until recently. We received this information from a very reliable source inside their organization. With enough money, you can buy pretty much anything."

"How did you get a picture of him so fast if he's new, and how did he become a general seemingly overnight?" pressed the chief.

"We're still not clear on many details, but they all came from our source."

After listening intently, the team commander, wearing lieutenant bars on his collar, piped up. "Not to sound rude here, ma'am, but this all seems like the intel just fell into your lap. It says here that this new terrorist cell is heavily financed, but from where? This feels like a rat trap to me."

"Gentlemen, you will have the full might of the U.S. military backing you. This will be a quick in-and-out to retrieve the target, and you should only meet light resistance," Victoria replied.

"Yeah, I heard that one before," grunted another SEAL. "Do you know how many 'light resistance' missions I've been on, lady?" Before Victoria could reply, he finished, "Not very damn many."

Mark knew the procedure and understood his job. He had already heard of this extremist, which is one of the reasons he was on the task force. Up until now, Umar Abdul had been a ghost, a nobody. But he was on the radar of the SEAL.

How did they finally get a picture of him? Abdul didn't seem to ever slip up, so why now? None of this sat well with Mark.

While Victoria continued the briefing, he started slipping out of the room to get a cup of coffee and begin the pre-flight of the Hughes OH-6 Cayuse helicopter he'd be flying to provide over-watch for the strike team. Just before exiting, Mark heard a question that made him halt.

"What does his tattoo represent?" one of the SEALs asked Victoria.

Mark paused for a moment, looked back long enough to see the insignia appear on the screen and hear Victoria start to say, "We're not sure, but we're seeing it branded on more..."

He left without hearing the rest. He'd never seen it before, but had his part of the mission memorized, and that's all that mattered to him.

"Just another radical regime that will come and go like the rest," he muttered as he walked down the stairs.

The operation would commence soon, so he wouldn't have much time to drink the green tea chai latte he was stopping to get at the little shop by the front of the terminal. This was his go-to drink, loaded with antioxidants.

Mark made small talk with the young brunette barista, making her laugh while talking about being stuck in Afghanistan.

"Doesn't being here make you feel like you're in jail?" asked Mark.

"Not really," she replied, smiling and batting her big brown eyes.

"You ever been?"

"Been where?"

"In jail?"

"No. Why, have you?" she questioned, eagerly raising her eyebrows and smiling even bigger.

"Would I score points with you if I had? Do you like bad boys?" Mark returned.

"Maybe," she confessed as her cheeks flushed and she giggled.

He left after a few minutes of banter and made his way over to the flight deck. He always wanted to see how far he could take a conversation, especially with someone he didn't know.

After approaching the helicopter and doing his walk-around, Mark climbed into the left seat while his co-pilot climbed aboard and looked over some paperwork. With his door on the Cayuse secured, Mark began to spool up the engine as his co-pilot looked everything over on his side and fastened the buckles around him.

They nodded at each other. Jim, a young, clean-shaven, tough-looking man with short blonde hair spoke into the mic on his headset, "How's the bird doing tonight?"

"She's doing pretty good. During start-up the fuel pump didn't want to turn on, so we're running the secondary one. I'll make note of it for the mechanics in the pre-flight," Mark replied, as he turned on the exterior lights.

He added throttle and collective slightly, and the Cayuse gently lifted from the pad and headed out to the runway.

"Kandahar Tower, this is Stray Dog, permission to taxi and take off," Mark requested of the tower.

"Stray Dog, Kandahar Tower, you are clear for taxi and take off," responded a crackly voice on the radio.

The Cayuse lined up on the runway, Mark aggressively added throttle and collective and the bird lifted off from the *terra ferma* and flew west toward the safe house, in the desert.

"Shutting off exterior lights," Jim said, as he flipped a series of switches on the overhead panel.

Mark dimmed the cockpit lighting system after he eased off the throttle, letting the aircraft descend closer to the hard deck. As they activated the Forward Looking Infrared (FLIR), a night-vision enhancement system built into the aircraft. The desert floor became visible and off to the right, they could see the convoy of HMMWVs with infrared (IR) beacons sparkling on the roof of each vehicle. As they got closer to the objective, Jim activated the video feed to record the mission from the air.

After about twenty minutes in the air, they were nearly there.

On the desert horizon a small house came into view. Mark eased off the throttle to decrease what little sound the low-flying helicopter was producing. Off to their right the HMMWV convoy had increased speed and was a few hundred meters from the safe house when AK-47 fire erupted from a window on the top floor. No return fire came from the convoy, since they didn't want to injure or kill the target. The HMMWVs crashed through the front gate and stopped in the courtyard. The SEAL team dismounted the vehicles, moved to the buildings and stacked up by the front doors, ready to breach.

The.50-caliber machine guns from the vehicle turrets answered enemy fire, shooting back toward the windows, but hitting only the walls. Bursts making *"thump-thump-thump"* sounds could be heard miles away. The intention was to slow the incoming fire as the team moved into position. More muzzle flashes lit up the area as the team got closer.

Mark maneuvered the Cayuse to orbit the outskirts of the safe house, and watched as the SEAL team detonated breaching explosives on the doors and entered the buildings. Flash-bangs could be seen going off inside as they cleared rooms. Even from a distance, the nova like flashes slightly interfered with their night vision in the helicopter. Occasionally, Mark took his eyes off the team to gain altitude in order to avoid sporadic small-arms fire from the insurgents on the ground and roof-tops. This stopped soon after the team took control of the building in the compound.

Once the SEAL team had entered the house and out buildings, the FLIR system in the cockpit of the aircraft picked up five bodies hastily exiting out the back door of the farthest building. Two people got into a large sedan in the front, while the other three entered an SUV behind the sedan. As the engines started up they barely glowed white on the screen.

"Right there, the SUV. Two men entered the front while one got into the back. That's Umar Abdul!" said Mark, after bringing the camera in for a closer look.

Jim keyed the microphone on the secure net.

"Control, this is Stray Dog. We have runners out the back of the safe house. Five in total and one is believed to be Umar Abdul. Please advise."

After a few seconds a voice replied.

"Stray Dog, this is Control. Hold your pattern around the safe house. You need to provide over-watch for the SEAL team until they extract."

Jim made a fist with each hand, then keyed the microphone again, "Control if we don't pursue we will lose them. Do you copy?"

"We copy, Stray Dog. We can't go off a hunch. If the SEAL team doesn't find anything ASAP telling us that it is Umar Abdul, we will go through the intel they find and proceed from there. Control out."

"The vehicles are leaving the area," said Jim, getting no response this time. "Control, this is Stray Dog," he repeated many times, until the radio finally lit up.

"You have your orders, Stray Dog, Control out."

Mark and Jim watched as the sedan and SUV sped off into the darkness with no head lights on.

"Shit, that was our boy. These head brass seem to care more about their procedures than winning the war," Mark mumbled to his co-pilot. "I'm done. I'm going back home and putting in for private-sector work. This mission puts the icing on the cake for me. Too many missions gone wrong, too many good men have been lost and for what, for some bureaucrat to look good and move up the chain of command faster? I need a break. I've heard about this top-notch place in Colorado."

The team on the ground eventually came out of the buildings and Mark was given the go-ahead to return to base.

The flight back was quiet except for normal radio traffic with command or Kandahar Tower. Neither Mark nor Jim were happy about how the mission had gone.

Once back at Kandahar Airfield with the Cayuse tied down, Mark headed directly for Victoria's office.

People moved out of his way, as they could see the man was on a mission.

"Victoria, who the hell was on the other end of the line in Control during the op?" he demanded, after pushing through the door with little effort.

Victoria glanced up, as she always did from her paperwork, not wanting to make eye contact. She sighed, but held her composure and responded, "Mark I know you're pissed about tonight, but..."

"I don't fucking care what you think. Answer my goddamn question!"

This time Victoria stared directly at Mark without flinching.

"His nametape said Joshua. He's been here a couple of days."

She went back to her paperwork as Mark stormed out of her office and headed for the museum that had been converted into the Mission Control center. Mark ripped the door open, filling the darkened room with bright exterior light.

"Which one of you fucking suits is Joshua?"

A man toward the far side of the room stood up and walked over to Mark. As he came closer his uniform became visible.

"I'm Col. Joshua. What can I do for you this morning, Mark?" he asked with a slight smirk on his face.

Mark was slightly stunned that he held such a high rank for someone so inept at directing field operations, but continued nonetheless.

"What the fuck is your problem?" This caught the attention of everyone in the room as Mark shouted right into the colonel's face, pelting him with saliva. "I had him! We've been after Umar Abdul since we first rolled into town, and then *you* let him just drive away!"

The Colonel attempted to maintain his cool.

"I'm your superior. I outrank you, which means you do as I say without fault and don't question it," he said.

Even if Joshua knew he was wrong, he wouldn't admit it and Mark knew this.

A huge grin grew across Mark's face.

"Oh, so that's how it is? No one is allowed to question you because it might interfere with your ass-kissing back in Washington?"

Mark grabbed for the colonel's blouse, ripping off the American flag and rank insignia that were attached with Velcro.

"You don't deserve to wear either of these," Mark declared, tossing them to the ground.

Col. Joshua made the mistake of making a fist at his side, which didn't go unnoticed by Mark.

The colonel attempted a punch. Mark blocked the throw, returned a swift punch to the gut, then knocked the colonel's feet out from under him with a leg sweep, sending him to the floor with a thud.

The colonel caught his breath and barked, "You son of a bitch, you're fired! You had better be on the next plane out of here!"

Mark threw his hands out to his sides and laughed. "You can't fire me because I fucking quit! If I had known I was going to be flying for the scenery alone, I might as well be taking tourists on fucking helicopter tours back in Alaska"

"You're a loose cannon, Mitchell," retorted the colonel from the floor, wanting to get in the last word and look as good as possible in front of his subordinates.

Mark had already left the room and was headed back to his trailer by the time anyone got to the colonel to help him up.

The after-action report would still be filed, detailing everything that had happened during the operation.

There was video and audio to back it up, but Mark didn't know if it would help anything. If it happened across the right desk, maybe they would see the error the colonel had made, but it was out of Mark's hands now.

Mark packed up his gear, which wasn't much, and turned the trailer keys over to Victoria.

"You know the Colonel's going to do everything in his power to make sure you don't get another job as a contractor...anywhere, don't you?" Victoria asked as he started to walk away.

Hesitating, Mark stopped and slowly turned to her. "I just need to take a break for awhile, and besides, what happens when the mission is gone over with a fine-tooth-comb, and one of the men that escaped was the target? Will it not matter then? I suppose we'll have to wait and see."

Being a civilian contractor had its perks beyond the scope of the military man. Mark loved his country and had served his time. He was, as they say in the Marine Corps, "Salty," and had "been there, done that." He was often looked at as an adrenaline junky. He was fearless in certain aspects. If it needed to be done to accomplish the mission, then Mark would get it done. He had been to most countries on the globe, even places most had never heard of, and he had tried to forget existed.

Mark's assignments were given to him by the task force to which he was attached, and he accepted them, never complaining, but sometimes questioning certain aspects. Even though he was paid more as a civilian, he still brought the same esprit de corps he did while on active duty. Doing the right thing meant just that. He and men like him did what needed to be done for God and county, not for medals or recognition.

Whether he was right or wrong about his position, he knew the game and that Victoria was right. Joshua would do whatever he could to ruin Mark's reputation. Mark left the room and said his goodbyes to the few people he gave a shit about before boarding a transport to Germany.

Trying not to let so many things consume him, thoughts of home and Christie filled his head.

Chapter Three

Fairbanks, Alaska
Fairbanks International Airport
Mark Mitchell, Ex-DOD contractor

Mark walked off the jet way behind the handful of passengers that had been on the plane with him and headed for the stairs to the lower level of Fairbanks International Airport to collect his bags. He wasn't in a big rush even though the trip had been a long one. He was glad to be home though, even if it was earlier than expected. With his reputation, he didn't need to look for work, someone would be calling him. There were plenty of jobs out there in the dark world that most people were oblivious to, and that's how Mark and men like him preferred it. In the mean-time, he would just enjoy the time off.

The weather outside was a moderate overcast of cumulous clouds floating low around the surrounding mountains and the wind could just barely be heard through the thick glass that overlooked the ramp and runway. Piles of snow could still be seen in some areas. It would be a little longer before it all melted.

Once at the bottom of the steps he saw Christie, his petite, five-foot-nothing strawberry-blonde, next-door neighbor, with his black, tan and amber German shepherd, Schnell, on a leash. As soon as the canine saw Mark, she tugged hard, pulling Christie toward him.

"What's up with the sunglasses? It's cloudy outside, and you're inside," Mark asked.

She tried to cover up a laugh, but failed and responded quietly while still smiling, "I'm faking being blind so I could bring Schnell in to see you. She's supposed to look like a seeing-eye dog."

Mark laughed, and then said, "Hozzam," to Schnell, one of many Hungarian commands she recognized. She came as she was instructed and Mark showed long-overdue attention to his dog to acknowledge her. They made their way to baggage claim, then out to the parking lot. They piled into Christie's VW Jetta and drove off.

Small talk was made on the short drive, and even though she wondered, Christie didn't ask why Mark was back earlier than expected.

"I've always been curious as to why you always wear that faded hat?" she did ask.

"What, this old thing?" Mark questioned, taking it off and looking at it.

"Yeah, I see new hats around your apartment, but you always have that one on."

"It's like a good-luck charm and it's never failed me."

Christie just smiled, not knowing how to respond.

They pulled into the driveway of the duplex Mark owned, on the side that Christie rented. Mark opened his door, then the rear car door to let Schnell out. She bolted out of the backseat and ran around in the yard playing with her leash like it was a toy. Mark carried his bags up to the front porch of his home and sat them down so he could unlock the door. As he thanked Christie for the ride, she paused as if wanting to say something, before walking into her apartment. Schnell heard the jingling of keys and, after relieving herself and re-marking her territory, came rushing to the front door with her leash and collar flapping in the wind.

Mark left the bags lying by the door after getting inside, took Schnell's leash off and turned on the television. FOX News came on. A female reporter was droning on about the crippled economy and increase in terrorist threats against America.

"Yeah, yeah, yeah," mumbled Mark as he walked into the kitchen to retrieve a beer from the fridge. "You've been rambling on about the same shit for the past ten years."

He walked back into the living room and flipped through the channels, settling on National Geographic. A show about exploring Antarctica was on. After taking a few minutes to walk around his house and check on everything, he sat down to watch it.

It was all how he'd left it seven months ago. The only décor on any of the white walls was a lone poster of Johnny Cash, a man Mark had always admired and respected, displayed crookedly above the couch. Christie had taken care of the apartment for him like she had in the past. He trusted her completely, and he compensated her with half off her rent each month. The duplex was paid for and he didn't really need the money. She had been renting from him for years, ever since she started college down the road, and he didn't mind helping her out.

Schnell jumped up on the couch, she started nuzzling his hand, then got down wagging her tail.

"Did you miss me girl?"

She let out a low growl, then whined.

"Okay, let's go for a walk."

Schnell walked over to the door and sat down anticipating her leash being put back on, while he put the beer back in the fridge. Mark put his coat on and then her leash. They walked out the door and proceeded to head to the little strip mall down the road. Schnell stopped a few times to sniff and even though she felt the tug on her collar, looked back to make sure he was still there.

They soon reached the coffee shop on the corner. Mark hooked the lead end of her leash on a pole outside and went in. There was no one else inside but the short red haired barista.

"What can I get for you?" she asked as he approached the counter.

Mark saw her name tag and said, "I'll have a green tea chai latte please Megan."

"Coming right up...," she paused wondering if he was going to offer his name.

"Mark," he replied.

She started making his drink while looking outside a few times.

"I love your dog Mark, oh, and what size drink?"

"Thanks, small please."

"Long hair German shepherd right, Eastern Europe?" Megan asked, as she handed him his drink minutes later.

"Yea, how'd you...?"

"Oh, I love dogs. I belong to a local organization, maybe you've heard of it? Arctic German Shepherd Rescue?"

"I may have."

"Do you mind?" She asked as she walked toward the door.

"She doesn't like everyone, please let me..."

Megan beat him to the door, opened it and said, "Heir."

Schnell just sat there looking at her.

"Okay, how about, "gyere ide."

Schnell walked over to her and Megan put her palm out for her to sniff, then let Megan pet her.

"I'm impressed," Mark said with a grin.

Megan smiled at him and said, "We see all kinds of service dogs, where did you get her?"

"I actually rescued her. It's a long story really."

"I'd love to hear it sometime. I'll be at the dog park down the road tomorrow afternoon, you should bring her to visit."

"I might just do that," Mark told her.

"Well, hey Mark, it was very nice to meet you both. I should close up now, my boss doesn't like me to get any overtime."

"Thanks for the coffee...Megan," he said with a smile.

Mark and Schnell started walking back down the road, when Mark spoke up. "What do you think girl? I think she likes you." *I think she likes me too,* he thought.

They got back to the apartment and Mark sat back down on the couch. Schnell laid her head in his lap and quickly went to sleep. Minutes later Mark was asleep as well.

Chapter Four

It was late morning as James Isaak stood very confused in the hangar. He was struggling to find a way to fit all of the cargo that lay strewn across the floor into the vintage Piper Super Cub. He took his cap off and rubbed the back of his short, brown hair for a few seconds then put the cap back on. Out of habit he reached up to pull on his beard, and when he felt baby-smooth skin, remembered he had recently shaved it off because of the upcoming time of year. "Looking professional makes for better business," he always said, so his winter facial hair always came off before the season.

James walked around the plane a few times before finally formulating a plan of attack.

Glenn Beck's syndicated program was playing in the background on an old dusty radio. Beck and his cronies were talking about how the economy is currently as bad as the Great Depression. The nation, as far as they were concerned, was on the tipping point, where it could worsen at a moment's notice and would affect the global economy when it happened.

James secured the large sheets of plywood he planned to transport under the aircraft's belly. A fifty-five gallon drum of avgas, aviation gasoline was strapped between the hull and wing support with a few ratchet straps.

"You'll have to ride up top," James grunted as he picked up a wolf he'd had mounted. He grabbed a long length of rope and climbed up a ladder. He set the wolf on the roof of the aircraft and grabbed the rope he had placed over his shoulder, arranged it over the mount and tossed the ends over either side of the plane.

"Andy, take those ends and tie them to the rings under the plane. Make sure they're very tight," he said to his son as he climbed down the ladder.

Andy was slightly taller than his dad. He showed off his extra height whenever he could, and this was no exception as he flipped his blonde hair out of his blue eyes and repositioned the wolf before tying it off.

"Now all we need to do is load up the Cessna 182 and we're good to go. We'll do that tonight when I get back. Let's go back up to the house and eat."

"Right behind you," Andy replied as James walked toward the house.

James stopped by the computer room to check the weather report before eating.

"I think I'm going to go ahead and fly the Cub over to the lodge in the morning while the weather's good, instead of tonight" James mentioned to Shelia and Andy while sitting down at the table for an early lunch. "Andy, that means you will need to load the 182 so it's ready to go when I return."

Andy nodded yes, with a mouthful of turkey sandwich.

"The first guests of the season arrive in eight days, is everything ready?" Shelia asked.

Shelia was a well-kept, intelligent woman. She was often referred to as the brains of the operation and the best-looking one in the family, and perhaps where Andy got his looks.

James shook his head no with a mouthful of chips, and then swallowed. "I still need to replace the cracked solar panel and do some wiring on the wind generator. That's why I'm going over a few days early."

They finished eating and got back to work.

Andy began loading the 182 early while James double-checked everything on the Cub.

Going across the inlet was an annual ritual and had been for as long as Andy could remember. The lodge was one of the premier places to stay on the west side of Cook Inlet, for tourists and fishermen alike. Like many jobs or businesses in Alaska, the lodge was seasonal, even though they could live there year-round. Andy was almost done with school and James and Shelia talked about moving over there full time once he graduated and went off to college. But for now this is what they did every spring until late fall, just before school started back up.

Just before he got in the truck and drove to town to get more supplies, James kissed Shelia, and gave Andy that look that meant *"get it all done right."*

The next morning, James woke up early as usual. He took a quick shower and grabbed some coffee before walking over to the hangar to get in the Cub and head over to the lodge. Shelia and Andy would be up soon, but the earlier he left, the sooner he could fly back and get them to fly over in the 182.

As he opened the big bay doors on the hangar, the sunrise could be seen peeking over the mountains on the Alaska Peninsula. Mount Redoubt and Mount Iliamna stood majestically above all else.

After belching a bit of black smoke, the old aircraft started right up and was soon rolling down the dirt runway of their property to take off.

As soon as he was airborne, James could see dark clouds on the horizon to the south and hoped that they would just pass by. The weather report was never completely accurate, and he knew that things could change in an instant in the Last Frontier.

Chapter Five

Fairbanks, Alaska
Mark Mitchell, Ex-DOD contractor

Mark and Schnell lay asleep on the couch. Unknown to them, the program on the National Geographic channel had switched off at some point in the early morning hours and the television was now broadcasting the FCC's Emergency Alert message as well as images. The volume on the television was turned down to a point that Mark couldn't hear it, but Schnell could, and the alarm sound made her whine.

With no warning and even less reason, the sound of gunfire could suddenly be heard outside which got their attention, although only slightly for the recently active-duty Marine. Schnell let out a low growl, waking Mark even more. He rolled over on his side slightly and mumbled to himself as he woke, "Damn Al-Qaeda, they always attack when I'm off duty."

He ran his hands through Schnell's glossy coat then abruptly stopped. "How'd you get here girl?" he asked, then sprang awake completely, knocking the coffee over he had gotten earlier and remembered where he was.

He stared in horror at the television, his mouth wide, as he rubbed his eyes. The footage on the screen was video from a cracked street camera, but it clearly showed a large blast going off on Wall Street.

The explosion took out the entire stock exchange, while the shockwave carried down several more blocks. Broken windows in buildings and cars could be seen, as well.

There was devastation and carnage all over the streets, scenes of large concrete blocks of rubble and bent and twisted steel girders. Strewn about in the ruins were body parts and blood - so much blood, pools of it. The people who survived the initial blast were only slightly better off, walking around dazed and confused, crying and moaning, some burned badly to a black char, while others were missing limbs. The transmission flickered. This time, photographs of the smoldering remains of the White House moved across the screen. Gone was the symbol of the presidency, the leader of the American people.

The attack was unprecedented, but ultimately inevitable, Mark thought. *The United States had stuck its nose in others' business for far too long.* He grabbed the remote control and switched through all the news channels. Each one was offline and only showed the same video and pictures. Repeating across the bottom was instructions to stay indoors, remain calm and obey orders given by federal, state and city officials.

Mark looked at his watch to check the time. It was just after 0530, which meant that the attacks took place in the early morning hours as most people slept, were headed to work or were at work already, depending on the part of the country.

"Sneaky bastards," he suggested faintly, as he got up off the couch to get his bearings. He wiped some of the dog hair off his shirt after noticing it clinging to his clothing.

A look of concern was growing across Mark's face, but his training as well as his will to survive were coming to life.

Full-auto gun fire from outside grew closer.

Smack-smack-smack! Was heard at the front of the duplex. More bullets could be heard hitting the structure as he made his way down the hallway, still half asleep.

Mark went to the gun safe bolted into his closet, spun the dial around and opened it, pulling out a select fire M4 carbine with a chopped barrel. In between the full-auto bursts of fire outside, he heard the reports from various types of weapons grouped together. He didn't know who was shooting, or why, but he was going to face them prepared for the worst.

He threw on his body armor and tactical vest, which already held loaded M4 and pistol magazines. He went to the front door where he'd left his bag, unzipped it and removed a small hard case. Pulling the key from his coat pocket, he opened the lock and grabbed his Glock, put in a loaded magazine and racked the slide. He grabbed a few more provisions and basic survival equipment, small rations and a navigational aid. He then put a round in the chamber of his carbine.

He picked up the phone in the kitchen. There was only a fast busy signal to be heard. He turned on his cell phone and it read "no service" at the top.

"All communication is down, girl," he said to Schnell, before hearing more bullets impact the outside of the house.

As he burst out the front door, he heard screaming coming from Christie's. After scanning the immediate area and seeing nothing critical, he ran across the front lawn, rifle at the ready, with Schnell on his heels. Mark noticed the door was kicked in. "Christie!" he shouted.

He heard another scream from the back of the house. He sprinted down the hallway and shouted again, "Christie, where are you?"

He went to her bedroom, stopped and listened as he scanned the room.

"Bathroom!" Christie shouted. Her voice was slightly muffled.

Mark jumped over the bed and moved quickly to the bathroom. A man, maybe in his mid-twenties wearing a sweatshirt with a hood as black as his intentions, had Christie cornered in the shower. He was holding the point of a kitchen knife between Christie's bare breasts, and her mouth was covered with his other hand. From the looks of it, he had caught her fully nude, completely by surprise. Mark instantly had the M4 carbine shouldered and aimed down the sights, with both eyes open. It would be a close shot, but this was how he was trained and it was the way he continued to shoot. As the attacker turned to face Mark, he let loose a four-round burst directly into the assailant's chest, after making sure his neighbor wasn't in the line of fire.

The sound was deafening in the small room. Some of the bullets passed through the man hitting and shattering the pink tile behind him, and coating them in a darker shade of red. The brass shell casings bounced off the wall and danced on the linoleum floor.

The man dropped like 20 pounds of shit in a 10-pound bag, Mark thought, as he watched the corpse slump against the wall by the shower. Mark grabbed

Christie's hand and pulled her up from the bottom of the stall where she was curled in a fetal position. She was in shock and could barely stand on her own. After he turned the shower off, even though she was all wet, he could see she was in tears. Schnell stood guard by the bedroom door while Christie was attended to.

He wrapped her in a towel and helped her out of the bathroom. He had her sit on the corner of her bed. She clung tightly to Mark while continuing to cry.

He forced her off of him and said, "it's all right, darlin'. He isn't a problem anymore. You're perfectly safe now. I'm not going anywhere."

Mark knew she wasn't in the right state of mind, but they didn't have time to hug and talk through what had just happened. He opened the closet door and dug around until he came across a rolling suitcase. He placed it on the bed next to Christie then went back into the bathroom, grabbing her toothbrush, toothpaste and some other miscellaneous toiletries that were laying around, and tossed it all in the bag.

He shut the bathroom door behind him, hiding the dead man, and began tearing through Christie's clothes while she sat on the bed weeping. He grabbed various clothes and underwear and dumped it all in the bag, except what she needed to put on. Moving the suitcase next to the dresser, he shoved the contents off the top into the bag as well.

He then helped Christie up off the bed, "Come on. Get up and get dressed, we have to go! We're leaving now!"

She did what she was told and got dressed quickly. Mark was facing down the hallway when, after a few moments, she put her hand on his shoulder to let him know she was ready.

He carried the suitcase in one hand and supported Christie by holding her up with her shoulder. His M4 rifle was attached to his vest and swung freely in front of him. On the way out he grabbed her coat from the coat rack and gave it to her.

"Put it on," he commanded, as he unplugged her cell phone and charger from the wall above the kitchen counter.

He slipped both into her pocket and they headed out the front door, back to Mark's place.

The door to his apartment was wide open and he heard footsteps and voices coming from inside. He set the suitcase down, shouldered his small rifle and slowly approached the door. The voices were coming from his bedroom. He motioned for Christie to wait in the living room with Schnell.

As he worked his way down the hallway, looking in each room, he heard Schnell growling deeply from the living room behind him. He stopped just outside the back bedroom and listened. He heard two men talking about killing Schnell first and then whoever else came through the door.

Instantly he jumped around the corner, carbine at the ready, and without hesitation double-tapped each of the intruders' center mass. They both fell to the floor as he scanned the room for any other threats.

After they fell, he knelt down by them and recognized them as the two college students renting a house together down the street.

"Hozzam," he said, calling Schnell over to him from down the hall.

Mark rubbed her ears in appreciation, and then stood up. She sniffed the men as he pulled the Remington 700 bolt-action rifle, chambered in .223 with a large scope on top, and the Benelli M2 12-gauge shotgun out of the gun safe, and propped them up in the hall. He also grabbed a Meyerco X-Ray 18 automatic folder with a 3 13/16 inch blade off the top shelf of the safe and clipped it inside his left pants pocket. He continued to pull freeze-dried food and Meals-Ready-To-Eat out from under the bed and placed them into a large black duffle bag.

He shut the bedroom door behind him and began moving the guns and supplies to the living room.

He asked Christie if she was all right. She shook her head from side to side.

Mark opened the hallway closet door and pulled out three large tubs. He pushed them over to the door leading to the garage then slid them down the steps to the garage floor.

The familiar sound of full-auto and miscellaneous return fire outside grew increasingly closer as he began loading gear. He dropped the tailgate on his King Cab Nissan Frontier, lifted the tubs in and shoved them all the way to the front. Next he picked up the three, five-gallon metal military gas-cans and strapped them in the bed, just behind the tailgate.

Back inside, Christie had partially regained her composure. She stood in the kitchen filling a cup from the sink.

Mark opened a cabinet and pulled out an armful of water bottles.

"Fill these up, as well," he said. "Glad to see you're back with us."

She just nodded. He picked up the duffle bag and weapons laying in the living room, carried them out to the truck and stuffed them in the backseat. After that, he picked up two fifty-pound bags of dog food and tossed them into the bed. Mark took several metal ammo cans off the top shelf in the garage and stuffed them in the backseat, too, covering them up with a few blankets and Schnell's extra bed.

He *whistled*, "Schnell! Come on, girl!"

Schnell came bounding from the living room, completely in tune to everything going on around her, but made sure to get what was important to her also. She was carrying a stuffed moose toy in her mouth as she left.

"In the back, come on, girl," Mark commanded, tapping on the front seat of the truck. Once she jumped in, she climbed onto her bed in the backseat.

Christie was filling up the last of the water bottles as Mark was loading his arms up with bottles of alcohol, wine, whiskey, vodka and a few without labels that were filled with a clear liquid. He sat them in a plastic crate on the rear floorboard in what little space was remaining.

"Where we're going, that'll be worth more than our silver and cash," he assured Christie as she was carrying a trash bag full of water bottles out to the truck.

She stuffed them in the backseat of the vehicle by Schnell.

"One more thing," Marked remembered, as he ran back inside to his office in the spare room.

He punched in the combination to a safe mounted in the floor under his desk and pulled out several small wooden boxes, assorted sizes of silver bars and gold coins, ranging from one ounce to one hundred ounces, then pulled the external hard drives from his computer and grabbed the laptop off the desk.

He stuffed all of it into a medium-sized backpack he pulled from the closet on the way back to the garage. He jumped into the Nissan and sat the bag in Christie's lap.

"What's this?" she asked Mark while trying to move the heavy backpack.

"Silver and gold bullion, Cuban cigars and some computer gear. They'll be really handy very soon."

She struggled with the weight of the bag and eventually let it fall to the floorboard.

Mark fired up the engine as he pushed the button on the remote to open the garage door, and said, "At least the electricity's still on for now."

Once the garage door opened, he pulled out. Out of habit he pushed the button again to close the door, and without stopping or looking back he floored the accelerator.

He drove down a few blocks, then turned by the strip mall he had been to the night before. A few blocks later, he they drove past a small row of houses and he saw someone lying in the street by a pool of blood that shown bright in the headlights. He slowed down and rolled past a woman with short red hair. *The barista?* He thought.

More gunfire could be heard, so he accelerated again.

They pulled out of the neighborhood and onto the main road leading to the highway. An Alaska State Trooper pickup truck with its lights on was riddled with bullet holes, leaving the windshield completely shot out as well as the tires, was parked on the corner. As they slowly drove by looking at the scene, a Trooper had been shot in the chest and head multiple times. He was in the passenger seat covered in his own blood and brain matter.

"He didn't even make it out of the truck," Mark said softly.

Another trooper lay on the ground in front of the vehicle. Almost nothing left to recognize the bloody mess as a human other than the uniform. The area around the truck was plastered with 5.56x45mm brass casings while several other assorted spent rifle casings and shotgun hulls were strewn across the street. The familiar smell of burnt gunpowder still lingered heavy in the cool morning air.

"Mark, why did someone kill those policemen?" Christie questioned, with her hand partially covering her mouth.

"There's no doubt that Martial Law is in effect. At this point they will have orders to go around and disarm all citizens." Mark paused for a moment. "Good luck with that," he said as he verbalized his thoughts, then gave the truck more power, then pulled away toward the on ramp to the AK-2 / Steese Highway. Mark headed toward Fox, a small town approximately ten miles northeast of Fairbanks, with a population of about four hundred.

Driving mostly on the shoulder, honking while weaving in and out of the very confused heavy traffic fleeing the city, Mark slowly made his way north.

After a few miles, they came upon the intersection of the Old Steese Highway and AK-2. Flashing red and blue lights filled the horizon.

About a mile out, Alaska State Troopers had set up a road block for a reason yet unknown to Mark.

Mark pulled the truck over to the shoulder once he got closer. He stepped out with a pair of binoculars, climbed up on a tire and gazed down the highway. They were turning most vehicles around and searching others. Shots could be heard and muzzle flashes seen, coming from the pullout where the troopers were searching the civilian vehicles.

He slipped back into the truck and stated, "Those stupid fuckers have no clue how to set a proper roadblock. There's at least five feet between each of their SUVs. We can blow through this one easily. We're not stopping and getting shot on the side of the road! It looks like people are getting shot up there, but I can't tell who's shooting who. Keep your body below the dash."

Mark grabbed Christie's shoulder and pushed her down toward the center console. "Stay below the dash until I say otherwise. You too, Schnell. Stay down girl."

Mark reached over to the top glove box, pulled out a 9mm Beretta 92A1 and stuffed it under his right leg by his groin. He put the truck back into drive and pulled away slowly, staying around forty miles per hour. He was still driving on the shoulder, waiting for the perfect moment when there would be no vehicles in front of him.

Once they were about fifty yards out, Mark rolled down the window and eased his left hand onto the grip of the Beretta. A trooper held his hand out signaling him to stop. Mark instead hit the gas.

The truck quickly reached sixty-five miles per hour as it clipped the two Ford Expeditions that were parked nose to nose in the intersection, directly forward of the front tires, flipping them out of the way with ease. They sped through the road-block, shots from behind thudding into the exterior of the truck.

On the right side of the truck, where Christie was hunched over screaming, a Trooper was taking aim with his Glock. Mark started swerving the vehicle while accelerating, hoping to avoid any bullets that might be heading their way.

Mark grabbed the M4 he had laying in the floorboard, raised it skyward, pointed it with his right hand out the back window and pulled the trigger. The magazine emptied, sending about twenty rounds soaring toward the stunned State Troopers behind them, keeping them pinned down. Mark and Christie sped off down the road with no one in pursuit.

Once they left the Troopers in the dust Christie sat up, faced Mark and asked, "Mark, what exactly is happening?"

Mark was silent for a moment, but before Christie could ask her question again, he said, "I have no idea. I woke up and the television was playing the FCC Emergency Alert message with video footage of a massive blast on Wall Street. It took out a few blocks when it went off. There were also pictures of smoking rubble where the White House used to be. None of what's going on now, with law enforcement, happened after 9/11, so this must be bad."

Mark reached for a knob on the dash, pushed it and the radio came on. The station was playing the same message that the television had been, advising people to stay inside, away from doors and windows and to listen to the radio or television for more information.

He clicked through all the FM channels only to find them playing the same message, so he swapped over to the AM channels and found the same thing.

"It's going to be a long drive without something to listen to," he said as he plugged in his iPod, which had migrated to the floor during the roadblock maneuver.

"*Karmageddon*" by Hank Williams III sauntered softly through the speakers.

While reaching for the line-in cord, Mark felt something wet on the console and turned on the interior light. Christie's jacket and shirt on her right side looked slick and saturated.

He slowed down and pulled into one of many turn outs on the highway, and said, "I need to get out and check something. It'll just be a moment."

Christie nodded as Mark stepped out of the truck and walked around the front. He noticed a small hole in the passenger door. He jumped into the bed of the truck, opened up the tub with a red duct tape cross on the lid and pulled out a small orange bag. He opened the pouch and pulled out a syringe and a smaller bag. He kept it tucked inside the palm of his hand and got back in the truck.

"Christie, you look like you're in shock. I'm going to give you something to help calm you down a bit. Just try and relax," Mark said in his most soothing voice, as he put the needle into her neck.

"Ow! What are you doing?"

At first, she struggled a bit, then she slowly went limp. After a few minutes she was completely out. He opened her jacket, pulled up her shirt, poured some Quick Clot on the wound to stop the bleeding, then taped a sterile bandage tightly to her side before continuing on.

"On the other side of this hill should be a truck stop," Mark mumbled to himself.

He drove for several more miles, then gave a sigh of relief as the truck stop appeared on the horizon. The parking lot was mostly vacant, and the sign by the road read NO FUEL SALES.

Mark pulled up by the door. An old man with a John Deere hat, a full gray beard and old greasy coveralls greeted him with the muzzle of a pump shotgun.

Mark slowly stepped out. The muzzle was tracing his every move.

The old man noticed Mark's dog tags hanging in front of him. He looked at them, then back up to meet Mark's eyes. At the same time, Mark noticed a faded anchor tattoo on the man's left forearm. There was instant recognition between the two men as there is with most military members.

Mark kept his hands away from his sides and said, "I don't want fuel. The girl's been shot and I need somewhere to treat her, that's all."

The old man kept the shotgun pointed at Mark while he walked over, looked in the window of the truck and saw Christie laying there in a blood-soaked shirt.

"Pull into the garage," he responded in a dry, raspy voice, before spitting.

As Mark got in the truck, a large garage door was opening. He backed in and shut the engine off. Mark opened the passenger door, knelt down, put his arm around Christie and picked her up.

Inside the truck stop, the old man had already covered a table with a tarp and set out a few bottles of disinfectant. Mark lay Christie down on the table and went back to the truck.

He called Schnell out from the back seat and climbed into the bed. He opened the tub that held medical supplies, dug around, and pulled out a large, bright-red bag, then went back into the truck stop lobby to attend to her wound.

Chapter Six

Lake Clark National Park, Alaska
Alaska Homestead Lodge
James, Shelia and Andy Isaak

James touched down in the Super Cub that morning after the short flight across the inlet. The sky above was clear, but far on the horizon, gathering gray clouds could be seen. He taxied the plane to where he normally parked, powered down the engine and tethered the aircraft on the railings they had made for this purpose.

He was unloading the Cub when the Park Ranger Matt Stevens, rumbled up on an old, dilapidated three-wheeler.

"Good to see you arrived safely. Are Shelia and Andy already here? I haven't heard from any of you in a few days," said the ranger, as James untied the wolf from the top of the plane.

"No, they're still on the other side. If this continues to get worse," he groaned, pointing at the clouds, "I'll fly back and get them in a day or two when we have better weather. We still have about a week until our first guests arrive."

"You don't know, do you?" asked the ranger.

"Know what?"

The ranger let out a sigh as he got off the three-wheeler and said, "James, there's been some kind of an attack. Wall Street and the White House no longer exist. The television stations are all off air, as well as radio. Best I can tell the United States is now under martial law."

James stood motionless next to the Cub then asked, "Is the..." he trailed off but the ranger finished the sentence for him.

"President dead? No word on that yet, but the White House was essentially flattened. Didn't look like much was left of it, from the pictures on the TV. I'm sure they moved him to some secret bunker somewhere."

James rushed up to the lodge, leaving the ranger outside by himself. He went to start the generators, then went to the main building. He made his way to the kitchen and picked up the hardwired satellite phone and dialed the number to his house on the other side of Cook Inlet. The phone rang a few times and there was a click, then dead air. He redialed, only to get a busy signal, then an "all circuits busy" recording.

As he kept redialing the phone, James noticed the park ranger was riding away on his three-wheeler. *Off to tell more people about the news, no doubt,* he thought.

He looked up at the taxidermied lynx resting on a log by one of the support beams in the kitchen and said, "Stop staring at me, I'm doing my best."

Between trying to call out, James went down to retrieve a few things out of the Cub for the night.

Andy can help get the rest once he gets over here, he thought.

James continued to watch the sky and try the phone throughout the remainder of the day. He kept contemplating getting back in the Cub and flying back home, but Andy knew how to fly the 182 and would bring Shelia over if it was that bad.

"I'll fly back in the morning if I can't reach them by then," he muttered.

It wasn't long before the sun was setting behind the snowcapped mountains, and it was getting difficult to see outside with the fading light and gathering clouds. He knew they would try to come over if they could, so he kept scanning the horizon with his binoculars from the top deck of the lodge.

Chapter Seven

Livengood, AK
Mark Mitchell, Ex-DOD contractor

Mark stood at the sink in the public bathroom. The door was open with the old man standing in the way with a blank look on his face.

"She'll be all right. The bullet went in one side and out the back. It's probably buried in the seat somewhere," Mark explained, as he tossed the blood-stained, blue latex gloves in the trash and began to wash his hands. "But I got her wounds clean and patched up."

"You two make a good couple," said the old man.

"No, no, we aren't, together," Mark corrected. "She's my neighbor."

The old man just laughed and started coughing as he walked into the lobby and placed his shotgun on the counter.

Mark walked out of the bathroom and noticed where the man had placed the shotgun. "You don't know how much longer power will be on. You should go ahead and prepare all of the frozen food so it won't be completely useless," Mark said while drying his hands on his shirt. "Not to mention I haven't eaten in about a day."

The old man went over to the limited frozen food section, removed a few frozen pizzas and placed them in the oven in the backroom.

Mark grabbed two bowls off a shelf, filled one with water and the other with Schnell's dog food from the truck. He called Schnell over and she began to eat without hesitation.

"By the way, what's your name?" Mark asked him.

"The name's Charlie. I was born and raised here." The old man coughed a few times and held his hand out to shake. It was a dirty, calloused palm, the hand of a working man.

Mark gave him a firm handshake and nodded. "Mark Mitchell, I'm a Department of Defense contractor. I just finished up my tour in Afghanistan, and returned home, then this mess happened a few hours later. Speak of the devil, would you have any details on what's happening, besides what was flashed across the TV?"

"I sure do," Charlie affirmed. "I got some info from my neighbor. He's got one of those fancy radios. The situation with the economy is worse than the Great Depression. Shortly after the stock market bottomed out, terrorists, probably Al-Qaeda, struck all across the United States in a coordinated attack on economic centers, government buildings, military bases, the works.

Whoever it was had a plan. New York has been hit several times and the same thing with Washington, D.C. The Pentagon is gone, too. Reports came in, and then the government shut them down and started broadcasting their emergency warning. Supposedly several military bases in California have been hit, also. I tried to bring it up on the computer, but the lines are down."

Mark thought for a moment. "I bet the satellite-based communications still work, but you'd still be unable to get through on a land-line or cell phone, unless you get lucky."

Charlie pulled a hammer and box of nails out from under the front counter. "Would you mind helping me board up the windows? Looks like I'm closing down for awhile."

Mark nodded. On the way to the garage he stopped by the back room where Christie lay asleep on a cot with a few blankets covering her. Schnell had dozed off by her side. Mark gently put his fingers against her neck, checking her pulse while gazing at the watch on his wrist. It was a weak pulse, but regular. She would recover, but it would be awhile.

Mark pushed the button to open the garage door, then helped Charlie carry out the large sheets of plywood and prop them along the front of the service station. He held the plywood from the bottom while Charlie put a nail in each top corner. They repeated the process until the all of the exposed glass was covered in plywood.

They both stood motionless, staring back toward the direction of Fox and Fairbanks before heading back inside. Smoke and a red glow from fires filled the horizon, and continuous reports of gun fire could be heard in the distance coming from all directions, echoing through the valleys and ravines.

"Can't go back the way I came," Mark contemplated, as he turned around, pointing up the road. "That leaves only one option, north."

In his mind, the most desolate, remote place was the best one. *The farther off the grid they could go, the better.*

After hearing the tell-tale *beep, beep, beep* of the oven timer, they returned to the lobby of the service station to eat the pizza the old man had cooked. Mild conversation took place over the next few hours. Neither of them had much to say, but both wanted to be friendly. They each nearly consumed a whole pizza by themselves.

Mark retrieved his rifle and a small bag with cleaning supplies and sat back down. He unloaded the rifle and his Beretta, then went to work setting out some cleaning supplies.

"Do you mind?" Charlie asked.

"Go ahead," Mark said, curious as to what might happen next.

Charlie grabbed Mark's M4 and quickly disassembled it then started to clean it.

"Done that before?" Mark asked him.

"A few times," Charlie said with a wink. "Been awhile though."

I knew there was something about this guy, Mark thought.

After both weapons were cleaned, Mark thanked Charlie and left him to his thoughts.

Mark surveyed the perimeter of the building from time to time. No other vehicles had stopped, and if any drove by on the highway, they would see the sign and boarded up windows. They would most likely pass on by at that point.

Later that evening, Mark checked on Christie again. She was still unconscious, but seemed to be doing better. Her pulse was stronger and all the rest would do her good. After one more perimeter sweep he unrolled a sleeping bag. He barred the door to the small back room with some old crates and eventually fell asleep on the floor next to the cot with all of his gear on.

Chapter Eight

Back in
Lake Clark National Park, Alaska
Alaska Homestead Lodge
James, Shelia and Andy Isaak

James continued to redial the number to the house in Soldotna for a few hours. Shortly after midnight he finally got through. The answering machine picked up and no one answered. He dialed again but the busy signal returned. After a few more attempts, he placed the phone back in its cradle, went downstairs and tried to get some sleep.

Falling asleep was hopeless. He tossed and turned for a couple of hours before getting out of bed. He had gone to the kitchen and begun to brew a pot of coffee when he heard in the distance the faint buzzing of an aircraft. He grabbed the binoculars off the window ledge, stepped out onto the wrap-around deck and began to scan the dark skies. Seeing nothing, he went back inside and sat down at the table, silent and motionless. He no more than sat down when the buzzing returned, so he grabbed the binoculars again and went back outside. He scanned the horizon but again saw nothing. The buzzing grew slightly louder. He sat the binoculars down on the ledge and stared into the sky, where slight, lower-level cloud cover could be seen in the moonlight.

He rushed back inside and went downstairs. He grabbed the flare gun and extra road flares then went outside to the crude road in front of the lodge that they used as a landing strip. He snapped open the flare gun, dropped in a flare and pointed it toward the sky. James pulled the trigger and with a pop the orange-red flare streaked skyward up through the clouds. He took the road flares from his back pocket, ignited the first and tossed it on the ground. He ignited the second and ran up the road and dropped it. He continued to do this until flares lined the edges of the road.

He dropped another shell into the flare gun and launched it skyward as the original flare died out, then pulled the final road flare out of his back pocket, ignited it and stood at the beginning of the chain of flares waving back and forth. The flare hissed and sputtered before being drowned out by prop noise from above. A few seconds later a white-and-blue Cessna 182 popped out of the clouds and descended toward the flare-lined road. The Cessna followed a shaky trail downward, drifting from side to side, speeding up then slowing down, gaining altitude then losing it. As it reached a few hundred feet from the ground, it began to lose speed.

James spun his hand wildly in the air above his head signaling to go around and try the approach again. As the Cessna passed by he saw Andy, his son, at the controls, but no Shelia.

James flapped his arms then held up two fingers in the light of the flare.

The Cessna flew over the flares, turned back toward the beach, flew down the shoreline, turned again and lined up with the landing strip. It slowed down and the flaps dropped two notches, and the Cessna came closer to the ground. The engine noise grew softer right before Andy pulled the throttle out to land.

James dropped the road flare and dove into the bushes by the cluster of birch trees next to the lodge to get out of the way. The Cessna touched down hard, and then bounced a few times. It touched down again as both main gears bounced back and forth. The nose wheel slammed onto the ground as the Cessna skidded to a stop. The engine throttled up a little and it turned and taxied up into the front lawn of the lodge next to the Super Cub.

James ran over to the plane as Andy was shutting it down and immediately noticed the bullet holes in the fuselage and windshield.

"Mom's been shot!" Andy announced franticly.

She was slumped in the passenger seat. They both grabbed her and took her inside to assess the injury in the light. Shelia's left arm and shirt sleeve were blood soaked as James carefully took off the layers of clothing. Andy handed James the towels he had run under hot water in the sink to clean Shelia's arm so he could assess how badly she was injured.

"It looks like she just caught a bullet fragment," he told Andy as he gently dug the small chunk of metal out of her arm with the point of his pocket-knife. She winced in pain and let out a fading scream.

"Is it bad?" Andy asked.

"It's superficial and looks worse than it is," James replied.

"She's going to be OK though, right?"

"Yes, she is. Who was shooting at the plane?"

"I don't know. Mom wanted to leave and head over here after she saw the broadcast on the TV, but we waited to see if you would come back. This morning she said it was up to us to get over here, so we got in the Cessna and took off in the darkness. After we took off I could see that something was wrong, as we gained altitude. There was smoke rising from different areas and not as many cars on the highway as usual. We were on our way over here, and we saw what looked like military ships in the water below. The sky above was filled with jets and helicopters. Out of nowhere, a strange-looking helicopter came straight at us and started shooting. It was like we were suddenly in the middle of a laser-light show. I banked hard left and dropped to one hundred feet as quickly as I could to avoid it, but we got hit. I never saw it again as we continued toward the west side, but mom had been hurt and I knew I needed to get here fast."

"You did great, son, now we need to figure out what's going on. Let's deal with her wound a little better, then we'll shut everything down that's not essential for right now. We can try to get some answers after that."

James knew they would be hard pressed to get any new information, but from his wide eyes and the pale color of his boy's face, James also knew he needed to reassure his son in that moment. He needed to outwardly show Andy that he wasn't scared and could handle what was going on, even though deep down inside, he wasn't sure everything was going to be OK ever again.

Chapter Nine

Livengood, AK
Day two
Mark Mitchell, Ex-DOD contractor

The alarm on Mark's watch rang at 0600. As he woke, he heard Schnell's claws clicking around on the floor while she explored her new surroundings. Mark stood up, yawned and stretched. He looked over and saw that Christie was still sleeping.

He went into the bathroom and took a very fast shower, then put on the same clothes and his Barrett cap, covering the short hair that had grown in since he shaved his head last. He whistled for Schnell to come as they headed for the garage. Mark took the M4 carbine out of the truck and swapped the magazine with a fresh one. He reloaded the empty mag and put it in the Boonie Packer redi-mag holder on the side of the weapon's receiver, in order to change them faster, and headed outside.

Schnell made her way to the bushes next to the building while Mark wandered around, surveying the area.

Looking toward Fairbanks, the horizon was almost completely pitch black with smoke. An amber light, like a fire burning to embers, was the only thing that could be made out. Tree tops above the light of the fires made them look like they were burning. The almost constant gun-fire that had been heard earlier now had turned to silence. The initial chaos, looting and revenge kills seemed to be over and now everyone was likely hunkered down, wondering what would happen next.

Mark called Schnell and they headed back inside. He stuck the chopped M4 back into the truck, checked the Beretta's mag and slid it on his belt.

He went to check on Christie, who was sitting on the edge of the cot when he walked in. "How are you feeling?" Mark asked as he offered her a water bottle.

"All right, I guess." She paused, "Considering what's going on."

She winced in pain as she tried to stand up.

"Easy does it, you're now a member of one of the most elite clubs around."

She looked confused then looked down at the bandages wrapped around her side.

"You got shot blowing through the barricade in Fox. I'm not sure if I'm used to it, or if I was in my zone, but I don't even remember the troopers firing any shots. Either way it was a clean impact, in one side and out the other. You'll be fine. A bit sore, but fine nonetheless. I suggest using the showers real quick. I'm not sure when we'll get to use one again," he said as he picked up Schnell's empty dishes. "I'll bring your suitcase in shortly."

Mark packed the sleeping bags and medical supplies back into the truck. He tossed a few one-ounce silver rounds on the counter, as well as a random bottle of liquor. He grabbed two bulk cases of bottled water and some energy bars and put them in the truck while Christie showered.

Charlie wasn't up yet, but Mark knew that what he left for payment would be sufficient.

When she came out of the shower, she heard the garage door being slid open. She dressed quickly with fresh clothes from her suitcase and went to the garage, where she found the truck packed up and ready to go. Mark tossed her one of the energy bars, loaded her bag and motioned with a nod to get in the truck.

They pulled out of the garage. Mark got out and closed the door, then drove off down the road. The cab of the truck was silent, void of conversation. The air was instead filled with the noise of the things rattling around in the bed, the tires across the rough dirt road and the stereo.

Mark was playing "Lost Highway," by Hank Williams.

Christie turned off the stereo. "You drive like a bat out of hell, you have military weapons and you treated a bullet wound," she said. "You're not a business consultant, are you?"

Mark drove on silently for a short time, then cleared his throat.

"No, I'm not. I'm a contractor for the Department of Defense, specifically in intelligence collection and counter terrorism. Most recently, anyway." Mark paused. "I'm sorry, but for the safety of both of us, I couldn't tell you before now."

They sat silently for a moment then Christie asked, "What was I suppose to do with Schnell if you never came back?"

"I imagined that you would keep her. That's the instruction I put in my will. I listed you as my emergency contact since my parents are dead and I have no next of kin, really, other than an ex-wife who wants nothing to do with me. I have a few friends who are mentioned to receive certain things, also. You've been very good to us and I was going to leave you most everything I had in this world."

Christie didn't know what to say, so she said nothing.

They drove on in silence for another twenty minutes, "May I read the will sometime?" she finally asked.

Mark nodded his head. "When things calm down," he agreed, while reaching for the dash to turn the stereo back on.

"You haven't even told me what's going on yet," Christie complained.

"What I already knew was confirmed last night by the old man at the service station assuming it's all true and accurate. People panicked and started rioting across the country after the attacks, so we fled and are on our way to Deadhorse. If things are this bad here, just think of how it would be in a large city. But Deadhorse, the way I figure it, is so remote and so far north, people won't be heading that direction, and the town itself only has around 50 residents, give or take a few hundred oilfield workers, so we'll head there until we can figure out a more long-term plan. I have a friend up there right now, as well."

After several hours of driving down a wash-board dirt road filled with potholes, Mark slowed down and pulled over. It was early afternoon now. He had been avoiding the bumps as best as he could, knowing it was taking its toll on Christie's wound.

"Coldfoot is just up the road and I want to check it out before just driving through," Mark said as he took the binoculars from the storage compartment on the bottom of the door. He stood on the doorjamb, propping himself up against the open door. He looked down the binoculars while swatting mosquitoes away with his free hand.

The interior of Alaska was always warmer this time of year, and it seemed the farther north you went, the larger the mosquitoes got.

"Looks clear, I see no movement from anywhere," Mark observed, before he stuffed the binoculars away in the center console of the truck.

He glanced down at the fuel gauge. It read between three-quarters and half a tank. He took one of the five-gallon cans from the back and filled the tank, then climbed back into the cab, slipped the transmission into drive and slowly headed down the road, keeping the speed around forty miles per hour. He reached into the glove box and stuffed the Beretta under his thigh.

As they pulled up to the small community of Coldfoot they saw an older, overweight man, wearing light-brown coveralls and a baseball cap with the gold and red *Shell* logo on it. He had a bitter look on his face as he stepped out from behind a partially-stripped pickup truck on the side of the road, but Mark was more focused on the fact that he was carrying an SKS rifle and had a 2-way radio clipped on his belt. He signaled for them to slow down and halt as the truck got closer.

Mark let off the gas and slowly came to a stop.

He rolled the window down as the man walked up and asked, "Where're you two headed?"

Mark kept a stern, aggressive look and informed him, "We're going to Deadhorse. We don't need any supplies, we just want to pass on through if it's all the same to you."

The man stared back and said nothing, two more similar looking men stepped in front of the Nissan, then the man with the SKS said, "Unfortunately for you, *we are* looking for some supplies."

Before the man could close his mouth Mark pulled out the Beretta and shot him in the face. A large chunk of his jaw disappeared while the back of his head blew out, scattering bits of brain and skull across the road.

Mark slammed the accelerator down. The rear tires instantly dug in and churned up dirt and gravel, forming it into a rooster tail of sharp rocks.

The truck rammed the man standing directly in front of them and clipped the third man, as he jumped out of the way, spinning him around. The Nissan lurched as the front man's body impacted the grill, and again when the tires crushed his torso. The gear in the truck bounced around as they rolled over him. The Nissan sped off down the road towards the horizon. Mark didn't even look back.

Christie sat in the passenger seat, dazed, staring out the window.

Mark suddenly thought of his cousin and her family on the Kenai Peninsula and wondered, *if all this is going on here, did James, Shelia and Andy make it over to the lodge before it all started?*

Shelia was Mark's third cousin, a distant relative, but family all the same. They had never really gotten to know each other until recent years, but Mark did accept an offer from her some time back to go spend a weekend at their lodge. Since then, Mark had spent more time with their family and Andy had become like a little brother to him. They would go hunting and fishing whenever they got together. If they had made it across Cook Inlet, Mark was confident they were safe from all the chaos.

After driving half the day, they finally came out of the Brooks Range. The exploratory oil wells and construction staging areas of Franklin Bluffs peeked over the horizon. After the shock from the incident at Coldfoot wore off, Christie had become less agitated, but Mark used the time during the drive to calm her down. Deadhorse was still about forty miles north. There was nothing but Arctic tundra and gravel road in front of them now.

"Where is everyone?" Christie asked, not seeing any vehicles as they continued down the road.

Chapter Ten

Mark and Christie
Deadhorse, Alaska

Mark dropped the magazine from his Beretta, slapped in a fully-loaded one and slowed down as they approached Deadhorse. A lone wolf in the distance caught his eye. It was walking on the rolling tundra to the northwest, padding steadily, its gray coat stood out from the miles of brownish-red grass and the occasional dwarf shrub. It was the only movement, and seemingly the only life moving for miles. The serenity of the area seemed as truly breathtaking as it looked in the pictures and as he had heard. He had never been this far north and, under better circumstances, Mark would have enjoyed soaking in the solitude, but not today.

"Are you seeing all this?" he asked Christie, who was still staring wide-eyed in a near catatonic state.

Many miles later, as Mark drove into the construction-filled area, he followed the signs to the police station office. It looked like business as usual, as men and women could be seen driving equipment and working. He pulled up to the front of a building and put the truck in park. He looked around the immediate area, doing a visual recon. Everything looked normal here, as if everyone was oblivious to what was happening in the rest of the country. Maybe they were.

"What the hell are you doing?" Christie screamed. "You just shot a bunch of people back in Fairbanks and now you are just going to walk into a police station, like it's no big deal?"

Mark grinned, "Yeah, that's the plan."

He stepped out of the truck into mud from the melting snow around the building, and took off his vest and leg holster. He removed his Glock from the holster, secured it in his waistband, under his body armor, put a jacket over everything then handed Christie the Beretta.

"Anyone comes near the truck, just shoot them," he advised calmly, knowing she wouldn't.

She took the gun and stared at him in disbelief. She watched him walk up the side stairs and disappear into the building, before setting it down on the seat beside her. He didn't think she would actually shoot anybody, but thought it might make her feel better to have it. He knew if the situation was reversed, he would feel better.

After several minutes, one of the two garage doors attached to the police station opened. Mark came out the front door of the office and walked down the stairs.

He got back into the truck and pulled the Nissan into the garage where a lone state trooper, with a rifle and gear similar to Mark's, stood waiting. He was tall and fit like Mark, but with short blonde hair and a clean-shaven, chiseled-looking chin.

After Mark pulled in, he slowly backed up then the trooper crossed his arms signaling to him that the truck was clear.

He put the truck into park, shut off the engine and took the Beretta from Christie, putting it back in the glove box. He stepped out, removed the body armor he was wearing and tossed it on the crumpled hood.

He then stood next to the trooper staring at the smashed-up front end of the truck, which was still covered in dried blood, while Christie sat shivering in the passenger seat.

"Looks like you had an interesting drive up," commented the trooper.

"I ran into a little resistance, but nothing I couldn't handle."

Mark signaled for Christie to exit the truck and join them, after a moment she opened the door and slowly stepped out.

"Christie, this is Travis Campbell," Mark smiled. "We go way back. I met him in Africa during Operation Desert Storm. He was a reserve Recon Marine from Echo Company 4th Recon stationed on Elmendorf Air Force Base in Anchorage, and I was a body guard for an ambassador. It's a funny story. Maybe I'll tell it over dinner."

"Very nice to meet you Christie. Let's go inside and you can tell me what's going on out there, Mark."

He was Mark's reason for moving to Alaska. Travis had grown up in the state and told Mark all about it during their time in combat theaters.

The two men had kept in touch over the years and had been on many hunts and outings together. They were like brothers in many ways. They drank and got into trouble, but always had each other's back.

Once in Travis's office, Mark spilled his story, minus his run-in with the troopers. Travis was a friend, but as a lawman, Mark didn't know how he would react to that bit of information. What Mark was able to share, made the current state of America a little clearer for Travis.

Mark still didn't have all the information, but it was a start. Knowing the United States was under attack from somebody using conventional weapons, not nuclear, was a relief.

"The satellite TV cut out some time ago and the technicians from Tel Com have been working on it. These interruptions happen sometimes and it always gets fixed really quickly. I had a feeling something was going on, so I ordered the borough police officers to be extra alert"

"Not going to happen this time, brother," Mark said. "Hell on Earth has arrived and it will eventually come to this frozen place, too. Just a matter of time til it does."

The three of them walked upstairs into the office area of the Arctic Police Department. Schnell stayed down below in the garage while they figured out what to do.

"I see you're still wearing that old Barrett hat of yours," commented Travis.

"I haven't gotten as much as a scratch on missions since I started wearing it," replied Mark with a grin.

Travis took his gear off and put his rifle in a secure rack, locking it. "It's time to eat," he said. "What do you two say? Are you hungry?"

They walked down a few corridors, got in a long line to dish up and continued to talk amongst each other.

The meal that night consisted of fried chicken, baked ham, mashed potatoes, white rice, green beans, corn and asparagus. Christie couldn't believe the salad bar that was laid out for them, as well.

She's still not back to normal, Mark thought, *but she seems to be shaking some of the shell-shock, since the situation this far north hasn't yet reached the boiling point like back in Fairbanks.*

"Is there some special occasion that's being celebrated tonight?" she asked Travis.

"Actually, this is one of the worst spreads that I've seen in sometime. The cooks must have changed out," he replied.

They filled their trays with food and sat down to eat. Christie continued to look around in amazement.

After dinner in the dining hall, Mark had Christie go and see the local medic. He knew he had done a good job in the field, but wanted a medical expert to look at her wound, just to be sure.

Meanwhile, Travis got the local officers together and let them know what was happening. Mark met them later to give them his account, again leaving out the part where he killed a few hostiles. *They might have a problem with that detail.*

A room was available down the hall from Travis's. He got a key from the front desk.

The next day they would have to contact everyone of authority in the area. The supervisors would be able to help them get the information to the masses. There were many people working in the area, spread out for a hundred miles in the various worksites, who would want to go home to their families once they found out what was happening out there. Cellular service remained down, but land-lines and two-way radios still worked. Many questions were already arising with the communications problem they currently faced, and no commercial or charter flights had arrived in two days.

"What're you going to tell everyone?" Mark asked Travis while they drank some bourbon and smoked cigars in the station.

"We tell them what we know and hope we can control what may happen. Ultimately, we can't stop anyone from leaving."

"What's going on?" Christie quietly asked as she walked in on the conversation.

"We were just discussing what we're going to do," replied Mark. "How did the visit to the medic go?"

"She said you did a good job, but I should go see a doctor or go to the hospital in Fairbanks or Anchorage soon."

"What did you tell her?"

"What could I say? I don't even fully understand what's happened in the last day."

"Why don't all of us just try to get some sleep," offered Travis. "I've set you guys up in a room with two beds. That OK?"

"It'll be just fine," Mark responded. "I'm going down to get Schnell and bring her up. Christie, I'll see you in the room."

They said their goodnights and went their separate ways. Mark soon arrived at the room he and Christie were sharing. After entering, he noticed her clothes on the closest bed to the window and heard the shower running. He set a bowl of food down by the door and waited to fill the other dish with water once the bathroom wasn't occupied.

Christie emerged from the bathroom, hair still wet, with a towel wrapped around her.

"Thank you for bringing up my bag," she said in a soft voice.

"Not a problem. I had to get my things, too. I'll leave for a few more minutes while you get dressed."

"I can just grab what I need and get dressed in the bathroom."

Christie took some clothes and was back out shortly in a long T-shirt and socks.

Schnell got off Mark's bed and jumped up on Christie's. She curled up, pointing away from Mark.

"Is she mad at you?"

"I don't think so. Maybe she just needs to get used to me again, or she senses what's happening."

"I know she missed you, she would run up to your door while you were gone and whine when she wasn't on a leash. I'm glad you're back too."

"I just wish it was under better circumstances. We better try and get some sleep, goodnight Christie."

"Goodnight Mark," she whispered.

Without any more discussion, Christie drifted off to sleep. They had been though a lot in the last 24 hours, so it wasn't hard for her to.

Did she just say she missed me? Mark thought, before falling asleep with his clothes still on.

The following morning, Travis, along with the help of the four borough police officers, went through the oilfields and made contact with the supervisors of the different oil companies and service companies in order to let everyone know what was going on. Without much information to go on, they knew it wouldn't be long before people would want to start heading south. They didn't have the means to stop them, but needed to have some kind of order, too. With supplies no longer heading north, the workers and other folk would soon be at a crossroads. They had the ability to make their own fuel, electricity and water, but not food. This would soon be a problem that would have to be dealt with right.

A meeting was set up with the supervisors who in turn would relay all information to their subordinates. In order to accommodate everyone, the meeting was scheduled to happen in one of the large hangars at the Deadhorse airport.

Chapter Eleven

That Night
Lake Clark National Park, Alaska
Alaska Homestead Lodge
James, Shelia and Andy Isaak

Once Shelia's arm was patched up, she went to bed, but couldn't fall asleep because she was still in shock. James took Andy out to the balcony and asked him to recount what had happened.

"I finished loading the 182 and was heading back to the house when I heard sonic booms from jets in the sky. I figured they were from Elmendorf Air Force Base and didn't think much of it. Mom came running out of the house and told me we were under attack. I went in and saw the news on the TV. We immediately got in the plane and left after grabbing some personal items. The rest you know."

"Did you see any markings on the helicopter or the naval ships in the inlet?" asked James.

"I was a little busy trying not to get shot down, Dad. But no, I don't think they had a flag or anything indentifying them, but I can't be sure."

"Okay, Andy, let's go get some sleep. We'll try and figure this all out in the morning."

The rest of the lights went out and the lodge was dark for the night.

James sat quietly, trying to get the computer and phone to work. He hoped he could get more information. He wanted desperately to know what was going on out there. Bright flashes of red-and-white lights followed by a few massive explosions that could be seen and heard in different areas on the east side of the inlet and he knew they weren't good.

Chapter Twelve

Earlier That Day
Cook Inlet, South central Alaska
Captain Yuri Korolev

The small foreign battle group making its way up Cook Inlet consisted of an aircraft carrier, a destroyer and a helicopter carrier that was nearly the length of three football fields. The ships were moving in to help quell any violence that might result from the recent collapse of the United States, as far as the sailors and soldiers on board were told, but their commander knew the truth of their mission. Capt. Korolev had served faithfully in the fleet since back when Gorbachev still led the Communist Party of the Soviet Union. Korolev had taken the post-Cold War fall of his homeland personally, much as he had for years before whenever he heard one of the capitalists from the West boast about the deal they got on their beloved, oil-rich Alaska. But now, with the decadent Americans finally reaping what they had sown, Korolev knew it was time to take back the land that should have always been Russia's.

"Captain, we're seeing more small aircraft flying around. Would you like to send troops in to the local airports and shut them down?" a sailor asked in Russian.

"Yes, I want light assault groups to land at these airports and at these vital areas," Korolev said as he pointed to circles on a map while talking to officers in battle-dressed uniforms that consisted of tan, brown and green digital camouflage. He was a barrel-chested man, with muscular arms to match, a tattoo on the right arm. His eyes were dark and his chin and jaw-line looked hard, as if they had been sculpted from marble.

"What are the Rules of Engagement, sir?" one of the men asked.

"Tell your men to only shoot people that don't comply, or resist with violence," asserted the captain. "The others will understand what to do after they see their friends and family die in front of them. I estimate all resistance will be brief."

"Sir, I thought we were just here to help these people?" asked the executive officer.

"Now that we have witnessed the destabilization of the United States we will take advantage and strike at the heart of the devil," he replied with a smug smile on his face.

"Is this sanctioned, sir?"

"From the top. Send the order," commanded Korolev.

"I will get the ROE out to all team commanders right away, sir," assured the sailor.

"Have all the AN/FPS-117 radar sites been located and destroyed?" Korolev asked.

"Reports of success have come in from most of our aircraft that were sent out on that mission and they report success, sir," replied a young officer.

"Very good. Let me know when they have all been eliminated."

"Yes sir."

"Captain, we just got word that an attack helicopter has fired on a small civilian aircraft and is reporting a mayday after the engagement," announced another sailor.

"Were they fired on by the aircraft first?"

"It sounds like it was flying straight at the helicopter and our men took it as hostile. They gave us the coordinates of where it was headed before they lost it in the fog."

"Can our helicopter make it back to the ship?" asked the captain.

"They say they should be able to."

"I want the pilot to report to the bridge as soon as they get onboard."

"Yes sir, Captain."

"Have you made contact with the United States forces in the area?" Korolev asked another sailor.

"Not yet sir," he replied.

"Keep trying to reach them. We need to make contact and give them our orders from the U.N."

"I will let you know the second I do, sir."

East side of Cook Inlet
Mile 20.5, Overlooking the Surf

"They're flying the United Nations and Russian flags, but are they friendly?" A skinny, blonde haired young man asked his freckly faced red haired friend. They watched with great concern as the large ships slowly moving through the water.

"They look like war ships to me buddy," he replied as he looked through his 10x50 power Nikon camouflaged binoculars, and then handed them over for a look.

"Maybe they're the ones that attacked us, like the TV showed," commented the red haired man with a dubious look on his face.

"We can't know for sure unless we ask them, but I for one don't want to get that close. Let's get to the cabin and load the rest of the rifle and pistol magazines, just in case."

The two young men went off to prepare for what they both knew was the inevitable, but hoped they were wrong.

There had been a few acts of random violence in town already and it was slowly increasing after martial law had been implemented by the troopers and city police.

"At least we have our own oil refinery and natural gas turbines powering the electrical grid," said red, as they walked along an old four-wheeler trail, avoiding the puddles covering it.

"Yeah, the heat and lights should stay on with no issues, for the time being anyway," replied the blonde.

What the two men saw, and would tell others shortly, was that there were aircraft patrolling the skies. Fixed-wings were all over at different altitudes and rotors were heading off in different directions from the ships. They witnessed the destroyer take up position closer to the east side of the inlet and the other two vessels toward the north. The aircraft carrier had moved into a position to launch more planes and helicopters. They had seen many take off already. Much was unknown since the TV stations had gone off the air, but what they would soon face was much worse than they could even imagine.

Chapter Thirteen

Lake Clark National Park, Alaska
Alaska Homestead Lodge
Day 3
James, Shelia and Andy Isaak

James woke up the next morning to the loud *whup-whup-whup*, sound of a helicopter approaching. After quickly waking Shelia, he went to the dining room where he saw Andy holding a plate with his half-eaten breakfast of bacon and eggs. The boy was looking out a large bay window at three military helicopters with strange markings that were landing on the road used as an airstrip for the Cub and 182. Men with rifles began running up to the house and down the road in both directions and up to the lodge. Their uniforms didn't look American, but James couldn't be sure.

As the large rotors were winding down the park ranger could be seen riding his old three-wheeler toward the aircrafts. Once he reached them, he was stopped by soldiers and Andy could see them engaged in conversation for a few minutes. The ranger looked as if he was yelling at them while pointing. He then turned and began heading back down the road. He didn't even see it coming. A few soldiers aimed their rifles at him and shot with bursts of automatic fire. The Isaaks' huddled together in fear. The park ranger fell off his three-wheeler and it crashed into some trees. Matt, the park ranger, but more importantly their friend, rolled a few times before coming to a stop. He wasn't moving anymore. His now lifeless body just lay in the sand as soldiers ran by him without a care for the innocent life they had just taken.

Shelia screamed when she saw the horrific scene unfold in front of her. Andy ran to the closet and got a Remington 12- gauge pump shotgun after he saw the ranger shot.

"Andy, put that back!" James directed. "We don't know who they are or why they shot Matt. We will greet them and offer our hospitality for now. Besides, a shotgun against all that firepower isn't going to do any good and would only make things worse."

James wanted to protect his family, but what could he do? *Maybe they will just leave after getting information, or maybe it was just Matt they wanted.*

Within minutes, they could hear footfalls on the steps leading up to the house. After telling Andy to make his way out the back and head to the hunting cabin by Silver Salmon Lakes, James went out front to meet them.

Shelia stood at the closest window as James approached the military troops making their way across the small deck. She could see unfamiliar patches and flags on the uniforms and the weapons didn't look like anything she had seen before. The men talked briefly before they all walked inside the lodge.

"What do they want?" Shelia asked James as they walked through the door.

"They want us to go with them," he replied, grabbing their coats off the rack by the door and handing Shelia hers.

More men filed through the door, pointing their AK-74Ms at the couple. Some of the men started walking through the house, checking for others.

The Isaak's did as they were told and followed the soldiers. Other people that they knew were filing down the road toward the beach at gunpoint also. Even an old man they only knew as Ted, a gentle soul who lived alone since his wife died a few years ago, was being helped along by others due to his back troubles.

As they all made their way to the beach, the Isaaks' could see more people from the small community being brought from their homes and lodges to a staging area past the helicopters. There were about twenty people living in the vicinity and all of them had been rounded up.

They were all told to stand in front of a small cliff and as soon as they did, a dozen armed troops moved in front of them. A soldier walked over to what looked like the man in charge and spoke to him for a brief moment. The soldier then spoke in Russian to a few other soldiers, who then went over and grabbed two young women from the group. There was a commotion and a few men were resisting now. No one knew what was happening. There was a lot of crying and screaming. While the women were being taken away, shots were fired in the air and the crowd fell silent.

A younger man stepped forward. "Where are you taking my wife?" he hesitantly questioned them.

A soldier walked up to him, pulled his sidearm from its holster and shot him in the head. The lifeless body fell, while blood poured out of the smoking head wound. The sand surrounding him was turning pink as the blood bubbled before soaking in. James started to shout something, but realized the soldiers had already made their decision. He turned to Shelia, whose cheeks had rivulets of tears flowing down them. He kissed her on the forehead and pulled her close. The commander gave the death squad of soldiers a few orders and they opened fire on the rest of the people who were standing there screaming, pleading for their lives. They all fell to the ground in a bloody mess as the two women, crying and screaming, were loaded on the transports.

The soldiers got back into the helicopters bearing Russian red stars outlined in whitet, and the choppers hovered while the door gunners on the beach side fired at the planes left on the ground, ripping them to shreds. They then flew back toward the ships as some of the planes caught fire and burned. Once in the air, they could see plumes of black smoke rising from different areas on the eastern peninsula.

Chapter Fourteen

Kenai, Alaska
Alaska Militia Forces and Army National Guard

A slight afternoon drizzle turned into a hard rain, as the first two Mi-26 Russian troop transport helicopters, carrying slightly more than one hundred seasoned combat soldiers each, touched down in a baseball field. As they ran down the ramps to secure the area, the soldiers splashed through puddles in low spots in the grass. The helicopters' massive rotors were stirring up debris in the vicinity and blowing over small trees. While securing the area, they met heavy resistance from the local populace. The Russian forces were armed with AK-74Ms chambered in 5.45x39 caliber and PKP belt-fed machine guns chambered in 7.62x54. The locals had hunting rifles, shotguns and AR-15-type rifles and many of them.

"We need reinforcements," yelled a frantic soldier on the radio as bullets could be heard *snapping* and *whizzing* by.

"Sir, the ground forces are asking for reinforcements," a sailor reported to Capt. Korolev.

"Re-route the attack helicopters to where they are needed. I want an accurate assessment of what is going on over there."

"Yes sir," replied the sailor, as he got back on the radio to coordinate efforts with the assault groups.

The scene unfolding on the streets of the all-American town was one that most people could never imagine. Russian troops were landing in transport helicopters and shooting unarmed civilians in the streets. Most of the locals quickly banded together to fight for their freedom. There had been acts of violence since martial law had been implemented, but it was now apparent to local law enforcement that they needed everyone they could get.

"LT, we have more helos inbound and the scouts say they are armed for bear," reported an overweight Army National Guard soldier who was clutching his M4 tightly. Sweat was running down the sides of his cheeks and his wide eyes showed how horrified he was.

"I want the rest of the Hummers to leave the armory and get over here ASAP to help finish these troops off, then we can deal with the next threat," instructed a tall, lean, young, Army officer who ducked as more enemy rounds impacted the car he was sheltering behind.

"Sir, they say they're still mounting the guns and loading ammo."

"Those men need to hurry! Dan, can you get some of your officers over there to assist my men?"

"They'll be there momentarily," advised the chief of police, while taking off his glasses and cleaning them on his shirt. He motioned to a few officers who were close by to go help. "Six months til retirement and this shit happens? That's just my luck. I thought we had early warning radar to avoid attacks like this. What happened to it?"

"That's a very good question," responded the lieutenant.

Two local police cars retreated from the road block they had set up at the end of the subdivision. They raced down the highway with great speed and as they got closer to the intersection and the armory came into view, the distinct *whup-whup-whup* sound of a massive aircraft could be heard.

A Ka-50 Black Shark Russian attack helicopter came into view from behind a group of trees. Its machine guns came to life, *growling* like a predator. The hail of bullets were its claws, ripping and shredding the pavement and everything in their path. The police cars stopped just as the bullets reached them, but the officers didn't have time to get out before the vehicles were torn apart by the 2A42 quick-firing, 30-mm machineguns. One second they were there. Then the next, only pink mist remained of the men. The cars caught fire, then quickly exploded.

Black smoke was rising from the vehicles after the initial explosion that also broke out windows in some nearby houses.

The helicopter continued to hover and scan the area for any more threats when it started taking on small-arms fire from below at its five-o'clock.

The Hummers at the National Guard Armory had opened fire with vehicle-mounted, .50 BMGs. The troops also shot their M4 rifles at the helicopter. The rounds were hitting it, but had little effect due to the armor plating. The aircraft was turning to engage the Hummers and men, when a rocket from an AT-4 anti-tank launcher hit its right engine and it banked left, then caught fire. It started gaining altitude and was moving out of the area when the rotors flew off, followed by the firing of the K-37-800, rocket-assisted ejection system as the pilot shot upward. His parachute immediately deployed once the rocket stopped propelling him up. The helicopter went down and exploded in the parking lot of a strip mall. It was witnessed by friend and foe alike in the vicinity. Some of the National Guard soldiers in the Hummers went to retrieve the pilot.

News of the attack helicopter being shot down reached the ship via some ground troops on the radio, which prompted Capt. Korolev to re-evaluate the attack options.

"I want our forces to take control of the situation. Tell them the ROE are now weapons free on all targets."

All of the sailors stopped what they were doing and a few questioned the order from the captain.

"Aren't we here to help these people?" asked an officer on the bridge.

Other sailors joined in asking similar questions.

Korolev paused to assess being questioned, then slowly drew his sidearm. A few sailors' eyes widened as he raised his weapon and shot the officer in the head. Silence followed as the others tried to process what they had just witnessed. The order was issued quickly by other sailors to the forces on the ground. Helicopters were engaging all moving targets regardless of whether they were attacking or not. Door gunners on the troop transports were mowing people down as the helicopters flew above the city. The jets were bombing all large buildings and bringing down all aircraft in the area that were trying to flee the madness.

Even with the airpower threat they now faced, the resistance from the locals was gaining momentum. More Russian aircraft were being brought down by small arms around the city as the fighting intensified. The ships closest to the east-side shore were taking small-arms fire from the bluffs above Cook Inlet, too. Anti-aircraft guns and the destroyer's massive main guns pummeled the coastline. They focused their fire on the areas that had structures and where they saw muzzle flashes.

Chapter Fifteen

Deadhorse, Alaska
Mark, Travis and Christie

The meeting for all the supervisors of the oilfields was finally being set in motion. With cell phones not working, the borough police had to use two-way radios and drive to many of the operation centers and individual housing areas, pre-fabricated modules built on man-made gravel pads. They went out to the places past the Deadhorse General Store, all the way out to the, "All this far and still no bar" sign at the other end of town, riddled with bullet holes by someone unhappy about being in a dry town.

Before Mark even walked through the open double doors leading into the hangar that had been designated as the meeting place, he could already hear the raised voices and shouting of an angry crowd.

"This looks like it's going to be interesting," Mark muttered to Travis as he casually walked up to him at the front of the building.

"They're all talking about just leaving. The last of the truckers to roll into town told many people of the horrors they had seen on the road getting here."

"You mind if I have a crack at 'em?"

"All yours brother. They won't listen to any of us, and we have guns."

Mark approached the small podium set up in front, pulled out his Glock and, fired a round into the air. It penetrated the metal roof, allowing a single ray of light to shine down in the dimness of the building. The angry mob stopped instantly and stared at him.

"Now that's better," he said, his voice echoing in the hangar. "Can everyone please take their seats so we can start this meeting like the civilized people we are?"

Travis walked up and grimaced at Mark, then put on a phony grin before turning around to face the crowd.

"I want to thank all of you for coming here today," he started. "We have a huge dilemma on our hands. The United States is under attack from unknown forces and we are cut off up here. My friend Mark here has arrived from Fairbanks and has told us that it's very bad down there. We don't know anything beyond that, so at this point we will need to shutdown all production and wait for further instructions."

Several people stood up and the yelling began again. Mark took out his pistol and was about to fire off another round when they all noticed him and stopped.

"My name's Steve Anderson and I represent BP in all of Prudhoe Bay," said a tall, thin man in a blue blazer. "May I ask some questions?"

"Yes, sir, please do," said Travis.

"You say that we are under attack, but have very little proof of this. Are we allowed to leave?"

"I wouldn't recommend it," Mark cautioned, "but no one will stop you."

"You said it's bad in Fairbanks, what is bad?"

"On our way out of town, we encountered dead people in the streets, roadblocks from law enforcement and civilians wanting your things and or your life."

"We?" asked Steve.

"My next-door neighbor left with me. When I woke up the other morning, I saw carnage on my TV. The White House and Wall Street had been destroyed. I don't know anything beyond what I've told you."

"Why did you come up here?"

"My friend is here," he said, looking at Travis. "And, this place is in the middle of nowhere. I was hoping that whatever is going on wouldn't reach such a remote place."

"We're going to have people wanting to leave and go to their families, if they haven't started to already," said another man wearing coveralls. "We want to leave and check on our families, too."

"This place is of strategic military importance and I'm confident that help will come," Travis assured them.

The yelling and questions started up again as people started leaving. There was nothing else to tell them. It had already been reported that people were heading south on the Dalton Highway out of Deadhorse. Mark and Travis walked out of the hangar and watched the vehicles drive away.

"What now?" Travis asked Mark.

"We wait and hope it's friendlies that get here first."

They got in Travis's Ford SUV and drove back to camp to check on Christie. They saw more and more vehicles leaving the area in a hurry.

Christie was up and playing cards with a few people when they found her in the lounge of the camp. Mark asked how she was doing.

"I've got some good pain medication and feel just fine, until I move too fast," she replied smiling. "How did the meeting go?"

"Like we anticipated it would. They didn't want to listen to us and will probably just end up leaving. Unfortunately, most of them won't last very long out there."

"That's a bad way to look at it."

"Just pointing out the obvious is all."

A few minutes later, a borough police officer walked in adrenalized and looking for Travis.

"People have come back into town and told us about a road block about sixty miles south at the base of the mountains made up of military vehicles."

"Were they friendly or did they fire on them?" Mark inquired.

"I don't think anyone got that close, but I don't know."

"Should we go investigate?"

"We can take the spotting scope I have in my office so we can keep our distance and evaluate the situation."

After getting their gear ready, the two men walked outside to Travis's SUV to make the trip. Just before they got to the vehicle Mark stopped and held his hand up with a fist signaling for Travis to stop.

"Do you hear that?"

"Hear what?" asked Travis.

"Planes. I hear planes," he announced while looking up, taking Travis by surprise.

They made their way to the front of the building and could see dozens of troop transports with parachutes deploying beneath them, flying in from the west. Helicopters could be seen flying in from the coastline to the north, as well.

"Those look like Antonov troop transports!" Mark exclaimed.

"Why would the Russians be dropping here?"

"Don't know and don't care. Either way, we need to come up with a plan, and fast!"

Mark and Travis watched as the unknown paratroopers landed all over Deadhorse. They both knew there would be panic and had to enlist help. More planes could be seen flying in from the south as they tried to get an idea of how many troops were being dropped. They went into the nearest construction camp's housing area, where people were franticly running through the halls, looking uneasily through the windows. Once they reached the kitchen area Travis asked loudly, in his Marine Corps voice, "Who can handle a weapon or has a military background?"

A dozen guys and a woman came forward.

"We're under possible attack by an unknown enemy," Mark said. "Right now, paratroopers and helicopters are landing around the area and we need help. We don't know for sure if they are friend or foe, but it looks like the latter."

"What are we supposed to fight back with?" asked a rowdy-looking woman with short hair and tattoos on her muscular arms.

"We have a cache of weapons and gear in the trucks outside," Travis revealed. "I know we won't be much against a sizeable force, but we may be the last line of defense for the North Slope."

At that point, a few people backed off and didn't want to get involved. Others stayed and wanted to help. Those who remained walked outside to either confront an enemy or to help Travis and Mark. They would soon find out which one.

Chapter Sixteen

Kenai Alaska
Civilians and U.S. soldiers
Fighting invaders

The Russian troops were taking heavy losses from local resistance, even though much of the town was already on fire or destroyed.

"Captain, we're meeting much aggression from the locals," informed a radio operator over the net. "They have much more firepower than we could have imagined and we are losing many men."

The only advantage they brought to the table was air power, until more American jets and Apache Assault helicopters from Fort Richardson and Elmendorf Air Force Base, both in Anchorage, had flown south into the area. The tables started to turn against the Russian invaders. The skies all around were full of tracer fire and explosions.

"I need more men on the north end of town," barked Ed Moore, the man who had stepped up when the chief of police and most of the town's officers had been killed in a recent air attack.

Ed had been an Army officer during the second Iraq War in 2003. He was a tall, lean man in his mid-forties and was being looked to for guidance from the others.

Ed took control and barked orders to the civilians who were willing to help.

Half a dozen men and women moved in the direction they were told to in order to re-enforce their fellow freedom fighters. None of them had any idea why they were being attacked, but they were going to fight for their very survival.

Bodies, both civilian and attacking military personnel could be seen all over the streets. The freedom fighters tried not to think about those who had been lost as they carefully moved to their destination. Some of the dead were blown into pieces and blood ran freely on the pavement and down drains, as if it had recently rained red.

This once-peaceful town was quickly taking on the look of a war-torn country on some other continent, far away. Machine-gun fire mixed in with small arms could be heard all around them as they made their way to help their fellow residents. Buildings were burning and cars and trucks were riddled with bullet holes. Broken glass from windows crunched underfoot all around them. As the group rounded the corner of another building, they came face to face with a few wounded Russian soldiers. A fast and furious firefight ensued. The popping sounds of semi and full-auto weapons rang out loudly in between the close structures. The smell of burnt powder and blood were the remnants of the encounter. Once the dust settled it had claimed the lives of all the wounded soldiers and three of the six-person civilian group. The carnage made one woman vomit as she fought to stand up using the butt of her rifle for support.

"We need to help them," she pleaded to the others.

"What can we do for them?" asked one of the men, who from the look of his waxy, parchment-white skin color, was in apparent shock, "They're all dead."

"We need to keep moving," argued an older man. "We can come back for them when this is all over."

The remaining members continued on to their objective. Once they got close they came across a make-shift casualty collection area in a parking lot between two buildings. Wounded U.S. troops were mixed among the civilians.

"What the hell's going on here?" asked Steve Robinson, an older man with short, salt-and-pepper hair, and a nicely groomed beard that was partially gray, too.

"We came under attack by helicopters as a large group of us were trying to get to shelter. These American soldiers just appeared and came to our aid," answered the woman, before walking away in a daze, clutching a blood-soaked wrap on a head wound.

Steve and the other two walked up to a soldier talking on a radio, hoping he was in charge.

"Excuse me sir," Steve said.

"I need you three to carefully move forward and help out on that road block over there that's under fire," he instructed, pointing down the road as he handed the radio back to a young soldier who was ducking every time he heard gunfire.

"Sir," started Steve. "Can you tell us why all of this is happening?"

As the soldier turned to speak, Steve could see a lone general star on his Kevlar helmet and on the front left side of his blouse was the name Bailey. The man was tall and had a thick black mustache. He spoke with the authority that his many years on active duty had taught him.

"All I can tell you is I woke up this morning and Fort Richardson was under attack and as far as I was told, the rest of the country, as well. Please help us win back this town and our country, if you are able. We need to take the fight to the enemy, and then once we've won we can find all the answers together."

"Yes, sir," acknowledged Steve, as he and his companions followed the general's orders.

Chapter Seventeen

**Meanwhile
Deadhorse, Alaska**

Mark, Travis and what seemed to him like a rag-tag team of go-getters, maneuvered in the direction of many parachutes that were landing some combat-ready troops. Weapons had been handed out to the volunteers based on what they said they could handle. There were only a few extra tactical vests to be worn, so many of the people were carrying extra magazines and ammo in their pockets. Most of the buildings were built on top of stilts so that the wind on the tundra could blow the snow through, instead of piling it up. The hard packed snow-berms slowed them as they had to continually look under the buildings for troops. A man who said he was good with a scope and knew how to shoot long distances got Mark's Remington 700 .223 sniper rifle. Others had shotguns and M4 rifles from the police station.

Just as they were getting into an ambush position for troops headed their way, explosions could be heard and felt. The rumble of the ordnance detonating was shaking the ground they were walking on, like mini earthquakes. The sky was lighting up with a mix of green and red tracer fire in the low light. Mark and Travis knew all too well what the colors meant, and had to explain it to the others, green for enemy and red for friendly. The team was set in place waiting for the soldiers to move into view once they unhooked from their parachutes. After the group started hearing explosions and more gunfire, Travis entered the nearest building and made his way to the roof. A few minutes later he came back down with some shocking news.

"There's C-141 American troop transports dropping paratroopers to the south and there is a massive dogfight going on in the sky west of here between many fighter aircraft. As far as I can see in all directions, the sky was full of tracer fire and air-to-air missiles. Planes and jets are on fire or exploding in mid-air," Travis told Mark and a few others.

"What the hell is going on?" wondered Mark out loud. "We need information. Take someone alive if you can. They may be U.S. troops, so don't fire unless I do."

Four soldiers were approaching a row of well houses that contained oil wells, when they came under attack by automatic fire from their right flank. The soldiers were cut down without having time to return fire. Soon afterward, the aggressors moved out of their hiding place to approach the bodies.

"Those are Russian troops," Mark whispered to Travis. "Everyone open fire when I do, but I just want you to wound them, so shoot for their legs."

Mark took aim down the sights of his M4, squeezed the trigger and dropped the man who looked like he was in charge, as he was pointing and talking to the others, with a perfect shot to his face. Blood splattered onto the men behind him as he fell to the ground, dead.

By taking out the leader, Mark hoped to cause confusion for the rest of them.

The small force was out in the open but had dropped to their knees and was returning fire, just like trained soldiers would do. Fire was exchanged between the two forces with bullets whizzing and snapping by the men. With cover and concealment aiding the small American force, the Russian threat was soon eliminated.

Mark and Travis told everyone else to stay put, and carefully walked up to the wounded and dead Russian troops hoping to get some answers. As they approached, a wounded soldier raised a handgun and was quickly shot by a distant weapon. The man with Mark's scoped rifle was covering them. Luckily there was one more wounded soldier left for questioning.

Travis turned quickly and motioned with his hand for them to stop shooting. He turned to Mark and said, "We shouldn't have let them shoot, or even have weapons, because they didn't listen very well."

"At least we have one left to try and get information from," he replied to Travis. "What are you doing here?" Mark asked the wounded soldier in a perfect Russian accent.

The man didn't respond, so Travis put the heel of his boot into one of the wounds in his leg. He screamed in pain.

"I will tell you what you want, just get me to a doctor in accordance with the Geneva Convention," he demanded.

"Geneva what?" asked Mark. "Listen, buddy, you people have attacked us, and there is no more Geneva to hide behind. Answer our questions and you'll die quickly. Why are you here and what do you want?"

Travis stepped on his wound again to get him to respond.

"Please stop," pleaded the soldier in English, but with a thick accent. "All I know is that we were told we were taking this land back for Russia. I was only following orders."

"Only following orders, huh? I've heard that one before. Where in Russia are you from? You have a strange accent," commented Mark.

"I come from the Upper Volga Region."

"Russian Orthodox?" asked Travis.

"Muslim," replied the soldier. "The will of Allah will punish all non-believers!" He let out a sinister laugh.

Mark pushed Travis out of the way and shot the wounded man in the head with his Glock.

"What the hell did you do that for?" questioned Travis.

The others in their group came out of their hiding places. As they were walking out they were told to halt by an American voice. Travis and Mark took to their knees and pointed their rifles in the direction of the sound. The others just stopped.

A squad of a dozen soldiers slowly walked toward them, appearing from between some well houses. Mark pointed up as Travis looked on. He could see snipers on top of the surrounding buildings.

"We're American soldiers sent here to help," said a shorter man, almost completely camouflaged in arctic patterns. He seemed in charge, being that he spoke with authority and no one else said anything. "Who might you people be... oilfield workers, maybe?"

"We're just concerned citizens lending a helping hand," Travis replied as he stood up. "I've enlisted these good people to help defend the area."

"We can use all the help we can get. I'm Capt. Jackson, 25th Infantry Division out of Fort Wainwright. We're moving from site to site eliminating all threats."

"Are these your men, Captain?" asked Mark, pointing at the four dead U.S. soldiers nearby.

"Not mine. They must be from another company and blown off course. Each unit had a drop zone, but the wind can cause problems for young troops like these. We need to continue on with our grid search-and-destroy mission. You are more than welcome to join us, but if you do, you will obey my orders."

"I have some things to take care of," Mark pointed out as he started taking grenades, magazines and AK-74 rifles off the dead Russian troops.

"Do you know what the hell's going on?" Travis asked Jackson.

"The only thing I know for sure is that the whole country is under attack, everything else is just speculation at this point."

Travis nodded and moved out of the soldier's way.

Capt. Jackson gave the word on his radio, signaling all his men to move forward. The snipers were still on the roof tops, covering the troop movement. From time-to-time, sporadic machine-gun and other small-arms fire could still be heard. The battle in the sky had pretty much subsided by now, and black smoke could be seen rising from many directions. A few soldiers took all the weapons and ammo off the dead Americans nearby before pressing on.

Based on what Travis and Mark could figure out from the situation they were now in, Russian troops were sent to take the oilfield, and soldiers from Fort

Wainwright, along with jets from Eielson Air Force Base, were sent north to take control of it, as well. The two forces were unknowingly sent on a collision course. Once they each reached their objectives all hell broke loose, in the sky, on land and at sea.

The Russian airborne troops, or "Vozdushno-desantnye voyska," were driving VDV buggie's, which look like a modified sand rail you would see on a beach or sand dunes, except that they had machine-guns attached to them. Due to the vehicle being mostly covered in armor, they were able to do a lot of damage to U.S. ground troops and civilians out in the open. The small vehicles were able to drive through the tundra and areas that Hummers couldn't go because they were too heavy.

Mark and Travis made their way back to the office to check on Christie and Schnell with a few of the civilians who didn't go with the soldiers. They met light resistance on the way back, and lost a couple of people before making it to the office.

The doors to the living quarters and offices had been barricaded by the inhabitants, so Travis went to the man door by the garage. He slipped his key into the knob and slowly turned it. He pulled the thick metal door open just as a shotgun blast peppered it and pushed him back. Travis quickly identified himself for whoever was inside shooting.

"Alaska State Trooper, hold your fire."

A borough police officer approached the door. "I'm real sorry, sir," apologized the young man in uniform, who was clearly shook up. It was James Harris, and the look of anxiety on his face showed his fear.

He was twenty-two years old, but looked like he was twelve.

"You did a good job," Travis declared as he took the shotgun from the officer, flipped the safety on and handed it back to him.

Mark and the others filed through the door. After closing it behind them, they heard screaming and then barking. Travis and Mark ran up the stairs in the direction of the commotion.

Chapter Eighteen

Deadhorse, Alaska
Housing Complex

Mark and Travis moved carefully, but as fast as they could, clearing the area leading toward the noise. After they got set, Mark would squeeze Travis's shoulder and follow him in as he entered. They took turns entering the different rooms in this manner. They covered each sector, overlapping fire for each other. After scaring a few people as they pointed their rifles at them, they reached the lounge and saw what was happening.

Schnell had a man in coveralls cornered. She was growling at him as Christie was slowly getting up off the floor while holding her side.

"What the hell is this?" asked Mark, furious at the man that Schnell was keeping at bay.

"He was saying that you and I brought all of this here," informed Christie. "I tried telling him it wasn't our fault, but he just continued to get more violent."

A few people nodded their heads, when the man in question tried to slip away down a hallway. Travis was on him in an instant.

"Just where do you think you're going, buddy?"

"I really want to get out of here and go back home," choked the slightly overweight, middle- aged man as he began to cry.

"None of us want to be here," Travis answered, "but we have to be strong for the ones that can't be. Now, man up and stop your whining!"

"Can I have one of your guns in case they get in here?"

"Hell no!" Mark exclaimed as he entered the conversation. "The last thing we need is friendly fire. Just keep the doors locked and barricaded. The Army is outside taking care of the threat."

"Is Christie okay?" asked Travis.

"This asshole tore her bandages off, so I'm going to get her to the medic."

"I'll meet you up there in a minute."

Even with all the fighting going on outside, the lights and heat were still on. This was a good thing, since it was still springtime and there was snow on the ground in many places, along with temperatures still dipping below freezing some nights.

Night was beginning to fall on the northern oil-field town. As it got darker, less gun fire could be heard. Travis was sitting near a window in an upstairs lounge next to their rooms when Mark walked in.

"You going to get some sleep, brother?" he asked.

"Someone needs to keep watch around here. I can take the first shift and come get you later if you want to spend some time with Christie."

"It's not like that, man. She was my neighbor and I was only looking out for her."

"Don't lie to me," Travis began. "I see the way you look at her. The only other things you treat that good are your dog and your favorite rifle."

"All right, I do think she's hot, but that's as far as I take it. She's more like a sister to me than anything."

"Well, brother, if this is the end of the world, I suggest you forget she's your sister," Travis said, smiling. "By the way, are you going to tell me what happened earlier with that soldier?"

"I'm still trying to figure this whole thing out, but when I do, you'll be the first to know."

Mark smacked Travis on the head then went to his room, where Christie and Schnell were already sleeping.

For the next few hours Travis sat looking through a window, and could see civilians and U.S. military troops moving around below. Sometimes a vehicle would drive by, but he would hear gunfire soon after it did. He knew there would be many more bodies by morning.

The wind was blowing in what looked to be a very aggressive storm. The clouds he could see outside hung low in the sky. A cold rain with snow mixed in began to fall, gently at first but quickly turned torrential, before letting up and passing a few hours later.

Just after midnight Travis went to wake Mark for his shift.

"Anything exciting going on?" Mark asked as he was relieving Travis.

"It's all quiet in the hood," Travis replied.

"See you in a few hours brother," Mark said as he took his post and Travis left.

One of the other officers that were still there would be taking the last shift at 0400 hours.

They were abruptly interrupted as they were getting around the next morning, when at a few minutes after 0600, machine-gun fire and explosions were rocking the rooms that Mark, Christie and Travis were in.

Bullets could be heard hitting the building and windows were shattering. Mark walked over, picked Christie up and carried her to the bathroom so she could avoid walking on the glass from the broken window. They all got dressed and geared up.

Travis walked briskly down the hall and saw the borough police officer on guard duty by the window. "Can you see anything down there?" he asked as the officer was straining to look out the window.

"All I can see is..." the officer started to say when a bullet punched through the window, hitting him in the head. Travis was standing so close to the officer that tiny shards of glass pelted his face, cutting it, as the bullet struck the window. Travis couldn't tell where the kill shot came from, since so many rounds could be heard being fired outside. It could have come from almost anywhere.

Travis backed up to the nearest wall as a few more rounds sailed through the window, shattering what was left of it. Mark, Christie and Schnell came up and crouched behind him.

"What's going on?" Mark asked.

"The officer at the window is dead. There's a sniper out there and I'm willing to bet he's not an American one. We need to get to the office and then down to the garage. There's a secure room down there."

The three of them crawled past the shattered window. There was blood splattered across the wall near the officer's body. Christie tried not to look as she moved past him. They made their way down the hall and into the dining area. Schnell was close behind. Many more bodies could be seen, and glass from the broken windows was all over the floor.

"It looks like snipers had a field day with all of these un-armed people," Mark speculated.

"It was bound to happen in a situation like this," replied Travis. "We should get some food while we're here."

Schnell was growling and looking at the kitchen. Mark told Christie to stay behind a turned-over table while they went to investigate. Travis followed Mark as Schnell led the way. The canine bolted forward growling, and screaming could be heard almost instantly. The two men turned their weapon lights on to see the commotion. A lone and wounded Russian soldier was cornered by the German shepherd. His uniform was soaked in blood on his right leg and on the left side of his abdomen. A pool of blood had gathered beneath him as he tried to stand in the corner. He had no idea how bad he was hurt and was clearly in shock.

"What are you doing in here?" Mark asked him.

"I...I was looking for food and shelter," he said.

"You're in the wrong place. In fact you're in the wrong country."

"Please help me."

"I'll help you," said Mark, as he screwed a silencer onto his Beretta 9mm and pointed the gun at the Russian's head. "Why are you here?"

"I was just following orders," said the wounded soldier. "I've only been in the army for a year. I just got out of airborne school and we dropped here. I don't know why, I was just following orders."

"He's not going to be able to tell us anything," Mark told Travis.

The two men agreed that what he was saying was true. The soldier was young and even though he was just following orders as he said, he was on American soil and he was the enemy.

Travis grabbed the soldier and escorted him to the nearest exit. Mark was right behind them. As soon as Travis opened the door and shoved the Russian into the opening, Mark put the pistol to his head and pulled the trigger once, *phoot*. As his lifeless body fell forward, machine- gun fire from an unknown combatant pelted the door and the soldier. After they shut it, a rocket propelled grenade hit the heavy steel door. The sound was deafening as the two men quickly retreated back to the kitchen to get supplies and move to the garage.

Chapter Nineteen

Prudhoe Bay Oilfield
Capt. Jackson, 25th Infantry Division

"Captain, I'm getting reports from other company radio operators that the Russians are moving west. They also say that many enemy snipers still remain around Deadhorse and are making it hard to clear the buildings," said a young soldier barely old enough to shave.

"Where's Colonel Morgan? Can you reach him?"

"I've heard chatter that he might be dead, sir."

"Who's in charge now?"

"I think you are, sir. Many officers are either dead or wounded."

"Broadcast this on all stations," Jackson ordered. "I want all troops to make their way to checkpoint Sally. They are to secure the position and carefully select targets. I don't want them shooting at anything but hostile forces. We need as many men as possible to assault through, building by building."

"Roger that, sir," acknowledged the soldier.

"Sgt. Evans, come here," Jackson told a soldier near him.

"Yes sir," replied the man in a deep voice.

"I want you to bring in the security from the flanks. Rally them in a staggered formation behind us. We'll be moving out soon."

"Yes sir."

Evans moved out with purpose to inform the rest of the men. Capt. Jackson got on his internal squad radio to order the snipers on adjacent buildings to link up.

"Firefly, this is Main, over," started Jackson.

"This is Firefly, go ahead, over."

"Firefly, I want your teams to move to the rally point. We're heading to checkpoint Sally momentarily."

"Roger that, Firefly out."

The three, two-man teams quietly packed up one at a time and made their way to link up with the rest of the company.

Heat waves were forming above the tundra, as pink, blue and yellow hues could be seen on the horizon. The now-smaller company moved to hook up with what was left of the division. With the sun coming up they all knew they would be exposed to sniper fire once again in the open tundra and gravel roads. The sniper teams were ordered to move ahead and provide cover for the rest of the men as they passed in a leap-frog style. If the main group came under enemy fire, the snipers would hopefully be able to eliminate it quickly.

The distant *pop-pop-pop-pop* of machine-gun fire could be heard more frequently as the bright orange globe brightened the day. Friendly sniper fire could be heard from the rear as the high-pitched, piercing whine of single overhead rounds cut through the still morning air, one at a time. They made their way closer to Deadhorse as the moon slowly disappeared and the sun got larger. They hadn't encountered any sizable resistance yet, but they all knew it was inevitable.

Chapter Twenty

Mark, Christie and Travis
Day 5
Deadhorse Police Station

After making it to the garage, Travis showed Christie a small room off to the side. There was a large vault door covering the entrance. He turned the lights on and handed her a flashlight, just in case the lights went out.

"This is the armory. It hasn't been used in years, but should be secure enough to protect you."

"What do you mean?" asked Christie with a bewildered look. "Are you leaving me?"

"We need to get back out there and get more information," Mark said. "You're in no condition to move very fast. We can't drive a truck, because it will attract too much attention. You'll be fine here and Schnell won't let anything happen to you."

Mark hugged Christie, which took her by surprise. She hugged him back and sighed. Travis showed her the safety lever on the inside wall that would let her out if she needed to leave. Otherwise they would let her out when they got back.

"Why is there a lever on the inside of the vault?" Mark asked as Travis shut it.

"I was told it was installed years ago after a young officer accidentally locked himself inside and died from asphyxiation."

"That would explain it."

Travis checked Mark's gear for him, and Mark, in turn, checked his. The men opened their bolts to make sure they had rounds in the chambers of both their rifles and handguns before leaving.

Mark stopped Travis as he walked toward the door.

"That thing yesterday, with the soldier... Something just isn't right about this whole situation."

"What do you mean?"

"The Russian soldier said he was Muslim and from what we know, terrorists may have bombed the U.S."

"Just because one enemy soldier is of a different faith, it doesn't mean that Al-Qaeda or another organization bombed our country."

"I know that," admitted Mark, "but I have a strange feeling about all of this. Things were really heating up before I left Afghanistan, which pointed to a major power play in the bad guy's realm."

"Try not to let it consume you. I need you fresh and alert out there."

Mark agreed and they walked out the man door by the garage while surveying the area. The men carefully made their way from vehicle to building at the same time. They stopped by a row of trucks in a parking lot to look at a pile of bodies on the other side of the road.

As they looked through binoculars, Travis spoke up. "So, what was that back there in the garage?"

"What was what?" questioned Mark.

"That hug you gave Christie? I thought she was 'like a sister?'"

"She is. That was to calm her down is all. Now, do you see what I see?" he asked, changing the subject.

"Yeah, a pile of bodies," Travis responded.

"They're not just civilian. Some are U.S. military too."

"This is the work of a sniper. He's luring them in to investigate, and if there are more than one he's just wounding them to draw more people in."

"So you're saying we need to find him, right?"

"Yep, and I think I know where the sadistic son of a bitch is, too."

Based on the way most of the bodies were laying, Mark explained that the sniper would have to be in one of the two buildings to the north. It would take them too much time to search all the rooms in both buildings, and if he was displacing on a regular basis, like a seasoned sniper does, it would be that much harder to find him.

"Are you still in good shape?" Mark asked Travis.

"Pretty good, why?"

"You think you can draw him out?"

"I can't out-run a bullet, but I think I can run fast enough for you to get a shot off. Just don't miss."

"I won't," Mark assured him. "You run in a zigzag toward the pile and take cover behind that Dumpster."

Travis got into position while Mark set up behind a Dumpster with a clear line of sight to both buildings. He squelched his radio twice to tell Travis to go and it was off to the races. As soon as he cleared the row of trucks he was running faster than he had in a while as adrenaline pulsed through his veins. While he made his way toward the pile, bullets started whizzing by him as he got closer. The sniper had a semi-auto rifle and was firing way too fast to be that accurate, but could get lucky.

"*Shoot, damn you!*" Travis yelled franticly.

Mark saw some faint muzzle flashes and smoke from burnt powder coming from about half way up the far left building. He aimed at the flashes and slowly squeezed the trigger, then again two seconds later, slightly to his left.

The shooting from the building stopped. Mark waited before he got up. He was sure he hit the sniper, but needed to wait to see if he was going to start shooting again. After a few minutes of stillness from the window, he was satisfied the shooter wasn't going to get back up. Mark stood up and started walking over to meet Travis to investigate why there were so many bodies in one area. They got their answer quickly as they looked over the carnage. There were two women in the pile. One was just barely sucking wind and a low moan emanated from her as she slowly drowned on her own blood. Some of the cadavers' eyes were still open and clouded with fixed pupils in the ghastly mountain of death.

Travis fished a rag out of his cargo pocket to cover his nose from the putrid aroma of decaying flesh. It was still early in the day, but the hot sun above them was cooking the corpses like the core of a nuclear reactor powering a city.

"Some of the men must have tried to rescue the women that had been hurt," Mark concluded. "They were used as bait to lure them in."

"What do we do about her?" Travis wondered, still winded from the run. Even with the rag covering his mouth, his hot breath could be seen each time he exhaled in the cool morning air.

"Nothing we can do," Mark admitted. "She's bled out and shouldn't even be breathing anymore."

"Did I hear you shoot twice? Did you miss the first time?"

"That was a textbook shot called a 'Hollywood,'" Mark said.

"Are you messing with me?"

"No, I'm serious. There was this guy that was in the same battalion, but a different company than me in boot camp a lifetime ago. He shot a perfect score on qualification day at Edson Range, and I missed it by one point. Long story short, he was a hell of a shot and taught shooting and tactics for years afterward. That was one of his signature shots for hitting an unknown target. You shoot where you last saw the flash, then move your point of aim to your left a few feet and shoot again two seconds later. Most people are right handed and will re-position to their right for another shot. It works most of the time."

"Very interesting," Travis expressed, still not sure if this was a line of bullshit or not. "What's his name?"

"James Perkins. Everyone called him Hollywood because he looked like a movie star, I guess, and he was in a commercial as a kid, too."

"Never heard of him. Do you think he's still alive?"

"I would bet on it," assured Mark. "He always had a knack for surviving sticky situations."

Mark and Travis took what gear they could off the bodies of the soldiers and continued on. As they approached a warehouse with a large pipe yard around it, they came under fire from what sounded like M4 rifles.

"Don't shoot back," Mark insisted, pulling Travis's rifle down as he was aiming in. "These should be friendly troops."

"How do we get them to stop shooting? And if they're friendly, why are they shooting at us?"

"They must be young or rattled troops to be shooting like that before identifying their target. Give me your Kevlar helmet."

Mark took Travis's helmet, put it on his M4 and slowly raised it up. The shooting stopped.

"Stop shooting, we're Americans!" he volunteered.

"How do we know for sure?"

"You don't, but I am speaking *damn* good English, aren't I? We're coming out, *don't* shoot!"

The men slowly got up and raised their hands in surrender with their rifles hanging in front of them and walked toward the warehouse. A few soldiers walked out pointing their weapons at them.

"Who are you?" asked a young skinny soldier with pimples on his face.

"U.S. Marines," replied Mark.

"Marines, huh. What're you guys doin' up here and why are there only two of you?" asked another soldier, with too much chew in his lip.

"That's on a need-to-know soldier," Travis informed him. "Now, we need to see your commander."

"That would be Capt. Jackson, and he's inside," said the first soldier.

The young man took them inside the dilapidated warehouse. There were soldiers everywhere and most of them either stood or gazed up when they walked in. They went to a far corner office where half dozen men were gathered around a table looking at a map of the Prudhoe Bay oilfield. They looked up when Travis, Mark and their escort walked over.

"Capt. Jackson, these Marines said they need to talk to you," muttered the soldier.

"And who are you?" he asked.

"Recon Marines on a top-secret mission, Captain. That's all we can tell you. We need to get any intel you have that will aid us in accomplishing it," Travis responded.

Mark looked over at his friend, impressed.

"How can I help you if I don't know what your mission is?" asked Jackson. "Wait, aren't you the men we encountered with the other civilians earlier?"

"You can start by telling us about Russian troop strength and areas they occupy," insisted Mark, trying to avoid the question.

"What rank are you two?" asked a lieutenant, the only other officer present.

"You're on a need-to-know basis, and you don't have authorization," explained Travis.

"Let's calm down here, men!" barked Jackson. "We're all on the same side. We've cleared these buildings and areas in blue, but the red ones are either occupied by enemy troops, or snipers, or both. We're going to be sending out platoon-size forces to take each of these areas one at a time with grenades and flash-bangs as they enter."

"I can tell you that this area here is secure," Mark informed them, pointing at a building in red.

"That one has a sniper in it. He's already killed a few of our men," announced an old and cantankerous master sergeant. with Burns on his name-tape, while staring the two newcomers down.

"We took care of him on our way here."

"We will verify that before just taking your word for it. Captain, why are we even talking to these two?"

"Please do. He's on the third floor, third window from the end. He'll be the dead guy in the room," said Travis as he gave the old soldier an icy glare.

"You should try Milk of Magnesia, Master Sgt.," Mark said.

"What's that, boy?" he targeted Mark with glaring eyes.

"It's just that you clearly have something stuck up your ass. Got me wondering if you were OK is all."

The other men in the room let out small chuckles while Burns' face turned beet red.

"Son of a bitch," he murmured.

"OK men, that's enough" Jackson interjected with a solemn look on his face while trying to hide a smile. "I know tensions are high all around but, *again*, we are all on the same side. We need to leave a security element here and use this warehouse as our casualty collection and evac point. I want sniper teams with each combat squad providing over-watch, and identify your targets before pulling the trigger. There are still many civilians out there. Let's get it done."

The soldiers started filing out of the room when Capt. Jackson spoke up again.

"Gentlemen," he added to Mark and Travis. "Most of the Russian troops have moved west. I'm assuming to take over the rest of the fields, but we've lost too many men to pursue them until we can secure this area of operation. A Marine unit has set up and secured the road south."

Jackson was pointing at a location on the map.

"Captain, do you have any information about who attacked us and why?" asked Mark. "All we got from our command before jumping in was an '*unknown, yet, well-trained* force.'"

"Unfortunately, I don't. We woke up yesterday and were put on high alert. The base was mobilized and all of the different units were given their missions shortly before deploying. All we were told was that the United States was under attack and we had to defend our area of operation at all costs."

"I was in Afghanistan hunting down Al-Qaeda insurgents five days ago. I have a hunch this was the largest terrorist attack in history. Thanks for the information, Captain, and good luck."

"Good luck to you men and your mission."

Mark and Travis thanked him again and left the building.

"At least we know we can travel out of here," Travis began.

"But why did the Marines set up a roadblock south and why does the Army not know what they're doing? We need to go talk to them."

"Let's get back and check on Christie, and then we can take my truck so we look official."

"Sounds good to me," replied Mark.

On the way back to the building, they encountered sporadic sniper and small-arms fire, as well as friendly forces, while they moved swiftly, sometimes running to get to cover.

Just before the men reached the building, Mark stopped them.

"Wait," he said to Travis. "Do you hear that?"

Once they stopped and controlled their breathing, Travis could hear it, too. Whistling sounds could be heard all around them.

The two men just stared at each other for a split second before realizing what was about to happen.

Chapter Twenty-One

Downtown Deadhorse, Alaska

"Incoming!" yelled Travis, pushing Mark aside as a bomb hit the building next to them, throwing up a thick wall of dust.

The two men ducked for cover behind a Dumpster as more explosions detonated, throwing dirt and shrapnel from buildings and vehicles all around.

The barrage only lasted for a few minutes but the devastation was immense. Buildings were flattened to rubble and trucks were burning. As they got to their feet, a lone man was spotted walking down the road, smoldering. He fell to the ground and stopped moving.

The building that housed the police station was only partially damaged. With the security of the walk-in armory Christie and Schnell should be just fine, Mark hoped. He and Travis quickly made their way into the building and methodically moved debris out of their way to get to the vault.

"Christie, can you hear me?" yelled Mark as he used a chunk of steel bar he found nearby to pry open the door that had been creased and damaged during the barrage.

"We're here," she responded, coughing.

Schnell was barking as Mark and Travis pushed the heavy door open just enough to let them out.

"We need to find a safer place than this to hole up," mentioned Mark.

"I know a place, if it's still standing," said Travis.

The trooper SUV was still operational, so they got in and drove down the shell-cratered road toward the general store, knowing they should be safer now in the vehicle with most of the enemy forces heading west. Travis explained that the building was an old one and had an underground storage room that was reinforced.

"Hey, look at that cute little dog. It looks lost," Christie offered as she pointed out a small white animal scurrying down the road in front of them.

"It's not a dog," said Travis, "It's an Arctic fox and, cute or not, most of them in this area have rabies, so try to avoid petting them."

As they got closer they saw that the gravel parking lot had many vehicles in it. Most of them were riddled with bullet holes or had been transformed into smoldering heaps of steel.

"Looks like other people had the same idea," Mark commented.

Travis slowly drove around to the back of the building and parked.

"Christie, stay here," Mark insisted.

With Schnell leading the way, the men exited the vehicle and stacked up outside the entrance. Finding the door locked they knocked to see if anyone was inside.

No one answered, so Travis walked back to the SUV and got a crowbar out of the back hatch. He jammed it into the door near the deadbolt and he and Mark pulled until the door opened. They turned on their weapon lights and slowly entered with Schnell directly in front. They searched the facility and came up empty.

"Someone was here," Travis concluded while looking at all the food wrappers and bedding material strewn across the floor.

"But, where did they go?" asked Mark.

"Maybe the Army evacuated them?"

"They still haven't secured the area completely, so where would they have taken them?"

"Guys, you better come look at this," Christie informed them as she entered the room, surprising them.

"You were supposed to stay in the truck," said Mark.

"I did, until I saw all the birds."

"What birds?" asked Travis.

"Just come and see."

Christie led them outside to the edge of the blood-soaked gravel pad. They looked out over the embankment and couldn't believe what they saw.

"That explains where all the people went," concluded Mark.

A mass open grave of oilfield workers and American soldiers was lying in the icy water below. All evidence led them to the same conclusion. The people were lined up and shot, and their lifeless bodies had fallen into the lake.

"Who would have done this, and why?" wondered Travis.

"I'm sure it was the Russians before they headed west, but I'm with you on why?"

They moved back into the building after they witnessed enough of the horror below.

"Can you believe all this is happening?" Mark asked, throwing over the table in front of him. "I left Afghanistan for this? At least over there we knew who we were fighting and why. Here it's a free for all. I was looking forward to taking a little time off and doing some fishing and hunting before getting back into the mix."

"I can understand your anger brother," Travis offered. "I was going to spend some time with my kids, and now I don't even know if they are safe, or still alive. Let's take care of business here and then we can get back to doing the things we want to do."

Mark regained his professional composure and focused back on the big picture. Christie was sitting on a mattress in the corner crying.

"We need to get up to that road block and try to get more information from the Marine element there," Mark suggested.

"We can't leave her here all alone," cautioned Travis. "Not after all she's been through."

"I don't want to bring her and possibly put her in more danger, but your right, we should stay together."

The three of them left to get back into the trooper SUV with Schnell close behind. Once they were in they made their way south to try and get some much-needed answers. For the most part the road was clear. There were a few gaping craters in the gravel road from exploded ordnance, and the occasional abandoned vehicle, but no signs of life. Many buildings and living quarters were either destroyed or still burning. No people, good or bad, could be seen as they drove through Deadhorse and onto the Dalton Highway.

"This is spooky," Travis whispered. "I never would have expected this place to be this deserted. With 24-hour operations going on, this place has never been a ghost town."

"I'd like to know how it's come to this." Christie blurted, taking Mark and Travis by surprise since she hadn't spoken most of the way.

"History is full of times like this in every civilization that has ever developed," replied Mark. "People eventually become greedy and they collapse what took hundreds of years to build. The Egyptians, the Romans."

"I know what history says. I am, or was in college. But why does it happen when it can simply be avoided?"

"Every time we went into combat, just following orders, we wondered that," said Travis. "What can we do to avoid being here or avoid shooting someone today? It's always on our minds, but there are always higher powers at work around us, pushing the limits and wanting things done. It's not fair, not good, but that's life and you just have to accept it."

"Wow," said Mark. "You're being really deep. Are you OK?"

"Checkpoint coming up," said Travis. "We can pull off up there and I can walk down to them."

"I can cover you from here, while still protecting Christie and Schnell."

"Roger that. I won't be long and then we can continue this conversation."

With that, Travis pulled over in a wide area of the road and got out to go confront the men at the roadblock. The truck was parked behind a small rise, concealing it, so Mark had to slowly make his way onto the road without being seen to cover Travis. Fifteen minutes later, he was almost there. Mark could see six Marines in camouflaged utilities behind a barricade made of two Hummers and sand bags.

Travis approached the troops and was immediately given directions, as soon as they noticed him walking toward the checkpoint.

"I need to talk to your commanding officer," he said.

Two men in full-combat gear approached with their M4 pointed at him, he could see the Marine Corps insignias on their uniforms.

"Semper Fi., Devil Dogs," called Travis.

They both stopped just short of him and looked at each other.

"Sir, please drop your weapons and gear and come with us," commanded one of the Marines as they got closer.

Without another word, Travis slowly did as he was asked, and after they picked up his things, he followed the men to a command tent that appeared hastily set up on a small gravel pad.

Travis was told to wait outside while being guarded by a few more Marines. After taking his tactical vest off he was only wearing body armor and his state trooper shirt. A couple of minutes later, a Marine major walked out and greeted him, then invited him inside.

"I'm Major Dixon, Second Recon. How can I help you, officer?"

"It's state trooper," Travis replied. "And, also Marine. I served in the Second Battalion 4th Marines on Camp Pendleton at camp..."

"Ahh, the magnificent bastards," interrupted the major. "I know the history of that unit well. What can I do for you, Devil Dog?"

"We need information," said Travis, slightly irritated at the arrogance of the major.

"What kind of information would you like? I happen to have quite a bit."

"How about, what the hell is going on in our country, who's attacking us and why?"

"All good questions. The 'who' is a very dedicated jihadist coalition consisting of Hezbollah and Al-Qaeda, as well as a few other groups. They hit high-value-targets simultaneously nation-wide five days ago. Here is a situational report that came in yesterday. It explains quite a bit as to 'how' and 'why' this is happening," he said, handing a paper to Travis as they walked through the command tent.

138

UNITED STATES MARINE CORPS

Major Dixon / Second Recon

IN REPLY REFER TO:

3574

S-3

DATE: April 22

1700

This terrorism plot was hatched in Iran at a 2010 meeting with Roshan Soleimani, the head of the Quds Forces; Umar Abdul, the operational head of Al-Qaeda; and Shideh Badr al-Din, the operational head of Hezbollah were in attendance with some members of the ultra-conservative branch of the Sunni Islam radical Wahibi sect that couldn't be identified.

The coalition, led by Soleimani, with Iran being the main source of funding, is based on a strategic collaboration and devoid of ideological differences and opinions of Shiite and Sunni Marjas. The main operational commanders are mostly well-known terrorists. They used proxies to hide this from us, but some of them talked after much persuasion by operatives recently. Based on intelligence and infiltration by Western agencies in the past few years, operations and cultural centers of radical Muslims have taken on a new face.

After 9/11, the new coalition started recruiting non-Arabs from many other nationalities to shift the blame away from them. Mainly "Islamic extremists," from countries not on the hot list for American agencies, so they could easily slip past security at all access points, mostly using student visas.

Terrorists had other cells take hostages in many hotels in large cities to shift authorities away from the real targets.

More than 4,000 targets were hit, many being public places, during high-volume times when people would be present, like malls or sporting events, government buildings, schools and military installations. Targets selected were clearly chosen to attain the most lethal effects.

This is the most up-to-date information we have.

Travis looked up from the paper in disbelief after a quick read and the major continued with more information.

"Why, you ask? They wanted to create instability in the U.S. and, well, all of North America, for that matter. I heard they hit Canada, too, so I think they achieved it. With all of the Mosques and Islamic centers built in the states recently, they had all the funding they needed right under our collective noses. Soon after the bombs were detonated and martial law was implemented, the United Nations troops were brought in to help us, but we've had to fight them, too, since they find us so vulnerable. Russia wants Alaska back, Mexico has invaded Texas, New Mexico, California, Arizona and Nevada, last I heard. I also heard a rumor that Cuba has attacked Florida, but I couldn't substantiate that one. Now, can I go back to planning my next mission?"

"Did we strike back against the enemy, sir?"

"We sure did, son, and we're not done by a long shot," said Dixon.

"Sir," interrupted a Marine as he walked in on the conversation. "Your sat com uplink is active."

"I need to take this, Devil Dog."

"Thank you for your time, sir," said Travis, prompting the major to turn back his way.

"These Marines will escort you back to the checkpoint. I suggest you go back into town and do whatever it is you do."

"I was policing the town, but the civilians are being slaughtered over there," Travis commented while pointing toward the town and construction area.

"The Army was brought in to deal with that threat. We have our separate mission and will complete it."

"Now, as a civilian authority, I'm going to ask you to link up with the Army and coordinate your efforts with them. Good day, sir."

Mark was waiting for Travis at the check-point when the Marines brought him back to the road. They gave Travis back his weapons and told them to leave.

"What the hell is going on?" Mark asked. "These guys wouldn't tell me anything."

"The Marine major in charge was pretty much stonewalling me, but he did say they weren't sent here to help the workers. That's the Army's job, just enough information to make me more curious. We need to follow them and see where they go. I read an interesting paper that the major said he got recently."

"What did it say?" asked Mark.

"It detailed how the enemy infiltrated the country and it had a few Arabic names that I couldn't pronounce."

"Interesting. I would've liked to have seen that."

The they walked back to the SUV and drove back toward town.

Travis put an iPod in a cradle at the bottom of the center console, and moments later, Metallica's, 'Wherever I May Roam' started playing.

The two men just looked at one another and nodded. A few minutes later the song was over and Travis shut off the music.

"I see you still have good taste in music."

"I thought it fitting, given the circumstances."

"Too true. Now, we can set up on top of one of the tallest buildings still standing," said Mark.

"The control tower at the airport would give us the best vantage point for miles around and we'll still be inside when night falls."

"Then that's where we go next."

Travis turned the iPod back on and a mix of music kept them occupied for the remainder of the drive.

Upon getting back into Deadhorse, they noticed more movement from the Army, which was a good sign.

After Mark and Travis secured the tall building, the three of them, along with Schnell, took what supplies they had left and moved into the lower level. Travis would take the first shift from the tower. Mark would make sure no one came in on the ground floor. A couple of hand-held 2 way radios were located in a downstairs office that would make it easier for them to communicate, since their radios were now dead from being on so long.

Before going upstairs, Mark asked Travis if he wanted a stim pill.

"A what pill?" questioned Travis.

"It's a drug the CIA developed for operatives on long missions. One pill can keep you awake and alert for up to thirty-six hours while enhancing your senses."

"What kind of side effects do they have?"

"None that I know of unless you take more than three of them consecutively," said Mark. "After that you can start hallucinating. Bleeding from the eyes, ears, nose and mouth have been known to happen, too, because of brain swelling."

"I think I'll pass."

"I'm on one right now," offered Mark. "It's been over 24 hours since I last slept and I'm fine."

"Still, I think *I'll* be just fine without it."

"Suit yourself, bro," Mark said before walking away to re-check the security of the building.

"How are you doing?" Mark asked Christie after they got settled in downstairs.

"I'm tired, hungry and my wound hurts."

"Why didn't you say something about any of that?"

"I didn't want to bother the two of you."

"Please don't ever feel that way again," Mark said as he got out some freeze-dried food and his cook stove. "You should wait until after you eat to take your meds."

"Why are you helping me and being so nice?"

"Because you've always helped me out and it's been good for both of us. At least I think so."

"All I did is rent from you and watch your dog. You don't owe me anything."

"I'm doing the right thing, I know that not everyone does, but I do."

"Works for me. What's for dinner?"

"Beef stew and raspberry crumble for dessert."

The two of them talked like never before as Mark made their meal, giving Christie some stew in a small pouch folded into a bowl.

"This isn't too bad," Christie announced as she choked it down making a face indicating disgust.

"It's not the best, but it does the job. You might like dessert a little more than the main course," he said with a smile.

After eating and taking her pain pills, she eventually nodded off and Mark watched out the windows while she slept.

Early the next morning, before his shift, Travis called Mark on the radio to head upstairs immediately. He saw movement on the road.

Mark looked at his watch. It was just before 0400.

Chapter Twenty-Two

Deadhorse Airport
Day 6
Mark and Travis

The Marines were moving to their destination, under the cover of darkness. Travis was watching them through a night-vision scope he had taken off an AK-74 rifle they had come across. Four Hummers had come down the highway and stopped in the parking lot of a hangar without a name. The whole property was fenced off and they accessed it through a gate by the road with signs that read, "Private Property" and "No Entry."

"What do you have?" asked Mark as he made it to the observation deck.

"Four Hummers and more than a dozen men just pulled up to that hangar," Travis replied as he handed the night vision over to Mark.

"Do you have any idea what's in there?"

"I don't, and there isn't a name on the building or on any signs. They all just say 'private property.'"

"We need to find out what they're up to."

"Let's go check it out."

They went downstairs to let Christie know what was going on. She wouldn't be happy about them leaving her again, but, being wounded, she would just be a liability if she tagged along if they encountered resistance. They woke her up to tell her what they were doing. She was still very scared, but understood the need for information. Mark secured her in a room with Schnell and the two men left the building. They carefully made their way to the hanger.

Once they reached the perimeter, Mark cut a hole in the fence with some wire cutters he had located in the tower, while Travis stood look out. They stealthily moved to the hangar and tried all of the doors, which they found locked.

"How the hell are we going to get in?" Travis asked Mark.

"We gotta pick a lock."

"Pick it with what?" he asked.

Mark produced a small lock-picking set and methodically went to work on a deadbolt while Travis stood guard. Within a minute Mark had the door open and they went in. They turned on their weapon lights so they could see in the pitch dark. What they saw were a couple of jets and vehicles, but no men. As they spread out to search the place, Mark noticed an office in the rear. He approached it and Travis was soon heading his direction from his left flank. There were a few desks and file cabinets inside, but that was it.

Mark opened one of the file drawers, then a few more and stated, "They're all empty."

"Why would they be empty?" asked Travis.

"It's a shadow room," said Mark.

"What's a shadow room?"

"It all looks legit, but it's hiding something else. Look for a secret passage or door."

"Are you serious?"

"I've seen the CIA and other government agencies use them to hide other rooms or areas," said Mark. "Trust me, there is one here somewhere."

The men searched the entire room and came up empty. They were about to give up, when the far left wall started to open. Mark hid behind a file cabinet and Travis ducked under a desk. A few men could be heard talking, and then walked out of the office. As soon as Mark and Travis heard the exterior door slam, signaling that the men had left the hangar, they moved to the wall, exposing an elevator. There was only one button, so Mark pushed it and the door opened. The console on the inside listed twenty sub-floors.

"Which one?" asked Travis.

Mark hit the S20 button while saying, "All the way down, then we can work our way up, one floor at a time."

The elevator moved with great speed and they were soon on the lowest level of a massive underground complex. When the door opened they walked out slowly and could see they were in a silo with very large missiles around them. They were alone. Water could be heard and seen dripping in many areas. The dank smell of a very old and moldy place filled their noses.

"What the hell are these doing here?" questioned Mark. "Did you know there were missile silos up here?"

"I didn't," Travis replied. "Are they what I think they are?"

"Yep. They look like intercontinental ballistic missiles."

The men looked around, then took some internal stairs to the upper levels. Most of the complex they saw below was storage space for provisions and weapons, according to what the door signs said. Once they reached Sub-level three they found long corridors with multiple rooms off to the sides. As they started to encounter people they moved into the shadows and rooms that weren't locked to avoid them. Level three had offices and meeting rooms. Travis had an idea that Mark didn't like.

"In order to find out what this place is, I can slip past these people with my trooper uniform on, as if I belong, and then locate a map pointing us to a control room or similar."

"I don't like it brother," said Mark. "You're just asking to get caught."

"It'll be OK man, I'm a state trooper," he reassured him with a wink.

Travis removed his tactical vest and handed it and his rifle to Mark, who slipped them into the shadows by a concrete support pillar.

Travis walked into a room that had a few people in it and did his best to fit in. He moved into a cubicle and sat at the desk with a computer monitor and keyboard on it. It was already switched on, so he began searching through files. None of it made sense, so he looked through the desk drawers and came up empty again. He got up slowly and turned around to leave, when he was confronted by two armed men in black BDUs and a man wearing a black suit jacket, matching pants, white shirt and a dark blue tie.

"Hello, Mr. Trooper," addressed the man. "Adam, will you please relieve this man of his weapons, so he can come with us, without incident?"

"Yes, sir," said a big clean-shaven man dressed all in black.

After his side-arm and duty belt were taken from him, as well as his pocket knife, Travis was hand-cuffed behind his back and escorted out of the room.

They entered another room down the hall and Travis was placed in a chair in the middle. The man in the suit spoke up. "Where is your friend?" he asked, with pomposity in his voice.

"I'm here alone," replied Travis.

"You two have been on our security camera screens since you cut a hole in the perimeter fence. Now where is he?"

"He was on Level two the last time I saw him."

The man motioned to a guard with a nod and he slipped out of the room.

"Why are you down here?" the man asked.

"Where are we, exactly?"

"Let's pretend you're not stupid Trooper... Campbell, is it?" he said as he looked at the name-tag on Travis's uniform.

"What is this place and who are you people?" Travis questioned the man while eyeing a strange-looking lapel pin on his jacket.

"I suppose it can't hurt telling you since, you won't be going anywhere. In the 60s, during the Cold War, massive underground caverns were discovered when drilling rigs kept hitting dead spots while oil and gas explorations were at their height on the North Slope above the Arctic Circle.

Investors, many of whom were wealthy and prominent politicians, had lost a large amount of money working with oil companies. Once the discovery was made, they got further involved with the Defense Department, in order to aid in the security of the country. The areas were reviewed with x-rays and determined to be viable for a system of silos as a first strike against the Soviet Union. The proximity to the country would allow for the United States to strike a massive blow in hopes that the enemy wouldn't have time to hit back. In order to pump the colossal amounts of concrete needed for construction into the caverns, drill rigs were moved on top of each area to facilitate this and hide it from Russian spy planes and anyone else on the surface. We have retro-fitted the old ICBM silos to house the current missile defense systems."

"I thought they were all at Fort Greely."

"That's what most people know to be true, including the enemy. That's why we have a secret and completely separate system in case of an attack, like the one that happened a few days ago. As soon as we have them online, we will be able to send them to their destinations. We have to hit back against the enemy, and this will make it so they don't bother us ever again."

"You could start a nuclear war!"

"They won't know what happened until it's too late," sneered the suit. "Our experts have assured us that the global fallout won't be an issue for the United States."

"You know that's not true, but you don't care because you're in a massive bunker and will survive," retorted Travis.

"We, along with other complexes like this, will re-shape the world after all of the evil is gone from it."

"You're insane, buddy!"

"Victor, please watch our new guest while I attend to other matters of more importance," the man said after touching his left ear, so that he could better hear the radio bud in it.

"Yes, sir," said Victor.

After the man left the room, Travis stealthily pulled his hide-a-key out of his pants and started un-cuffing himself.

"So... Victor, can I call you Victor? What's with all of you apes working security down here? I haven't seen so much hair on men before. Did they breed you in a lab? You all look the same, all muscles, hair and no brains."

"Listen here, little man," began Victor as he approached Travis.

Travis was free of his cuffs, but kept taunting the oversized man drawing him in. When he got within a few feet, Travis made his move.

Chapter Twenty-Three

In Contact Underground
Mark and Travis

Victor closed in and Travis sprang out of the chair, taking him by surprise. As Victor reached for his side-arm Travis jumped in the air hitting him in the chest with both feet. This knocked the large man off balance and he fell backward. Travis hit the floor with a thud, then rolled to his side and grabbed the chair as he got up. He raised it over his head and slammed it down on Victor. The blow from the chair knocked his handgun away. Victor rolled over and got up taking the chair away from Travis, while grabbing his throat and lifting him off the ground. Using his force to slam Travis into the far wall, Travis flew across the room in the direction of the pistol. After hitting the floor and rolling to a stop, Travis gathered his senses enough to see the handgun next to him. He picked it up while an angry Victor ran at him. Travis quickly aimed and fired one round. The large man was hit in the head with the .45 caliber round from his own 1911. He hit the floor and his forward momentum sent him sliding to Travis's feet. Blood poured from the large wound on Victor's head. Travis gathered a few items off the man, like an AL Mar Auto SERE knife with a 3.5 inch blade and some extra magazines for the handgun. After getting what he could, Travis left the room to look for Mark.

After they got separated, Mark was looking for Travis when he came across the observation deck of some sort of command and control center. The massive computer screens were displaying, with crystal clarity, what looked like satellite imagery. He could see that much of the United Stated as well as Canada had been attacked. Different countries on the map display were blacked out too like England, France, Germany and several more European countries. What this meant was still unknown. Were they destroyed or were they targets for the ICBMs?

"What the hell is going on?" Mark quietly asked himself.

There were over a dozen people in the room at different consoles. A smaller screen had live images of the missile silos with the radiation symbol on it. This was the one that concerned Mark the most.

"If the United States had been devastated that badly, and many other countries are destroyed, too, this could be the beginning of World War III. I can't let them launch those nukes," Mark thought, as he left the room.

Travis was carefully making his way back to the area where he had left Mark, when he rounded a corner and ran right into one of the complex's security guards, an athletic-looking thug dressed in all black. The two men instantly pushed each other back and pulled side-arms. Travis moved in and knocked the other man's gun from his hands. The guard chopped Travis's hand, making him drop his weapon, too. Travis pulled the knife he had lifted off Victor and started stabbing and slicing as the man blocked all advances while backing up.

The security guard pulled a knife as well. Travis couldn't see exactly what kind or size it was, in the poorly lit corridor. Regardless, he heard the blade pop out, an auto-folder from the sound and the man advanced forward, slowly moving to his right, looking for an in. Travis was hit with a fast jab once in his left arm while he was figuring out the man's moves. The guard faked a stab, then tried to kick Travis's leg, which was a mistake. Travis quickly countered and lunged, cutting the man near his groin. This hurt the man badly, maybe even slicing his femoral artery. The man attacked and steel met steel as both men sliced and poked. They met close again and Travis was able to slice the man's wrist that held his knife. This caused him to drop it and attack with both fists. The blood from the guards leg wound was making the floor slippery in spots and made both men move in unison to avoid any puddles.

They were well trained in hand-to-hand combat and were both at a disadvantage as they fought. It was as if they were anticipating every move the other threw out. The guard was trying desperately to get the knife out of Travis's hand. He was blocking it, while kicking and kneeing, with nothing contacting the right places as Travis blocked them, too.

"You're pretty good, big boy," taunted Travis.

"I'm going to show you just how good when I take that knife and bleed you like a pig!"

"I'd like to see you try, hotrod!"

While the minutes of hand-to-hand fighting ticked by, Travis continued his attack and eventually got the upper hand, locking arms with the guard. Travis sent a knee into the man's leg wound, which made the man loosen his grip as he writhed in agony. Travis dropped the knife out of his right hand, and it fell into his left. With a hard upward stroke, he drove it through the guard's throat and into his mouth. Blood instantly started spraying out of the large knife wound as the severed artery pulsed rhythmically with the last beats of his heart. Travis set him down quietly while pulling the blade out.

"You weren't good enough, buddy," Travis said as he wiped the blood from the knife onto the man's pants.

Despite the noise, no one else came. Travis quickly moved the body into the shadows. He located both handguns and continued down the hall.

Chapter Twenty-Four

Deadhorse, Alaska
Capt. Jackson, 25th Infantry Division

"Captain, we've cleared this entire sector," said Master Sgt. Burns, pointing at a map on a desk inside the old warehouse that had been converted to a command post and casualty collection point.

"That's good news," declared Jackson. "I need an accurate assessment of all the men and supplies we have at our disposal. If this area is secured, then we need to move west in pursuit of the Russian army."

"But sir, we don't have those orders."

"Without being able to contact Interior Command, we need to improvise and destroy the enemy. You have your orders, Burns."

"Yes, sir. Let's go men," he said as he left the small office.

A few soldiers followed Burns to go get the Captain the information he needed.

They had taken heavy losses for only having fought for five days. Without air support and artillery to help them, they had nothing but each other to rely on. Many of the wounded had died. Most of the medics had been lost and with no medivacs to take the men to a hospital, many just succumbed to their wounds.

Forty minutes later Master Sgt. Burns returned to find Cpt. Jackson asleep at the desk in the corner.

He knew he should wake him, but instead made a command decision to let him and many of the other soldiers get some well-needed rest. After issuing orders for outside security and a rotation, he sat down outside the office and eventually fell asleep himself.

Chapter Twenty-Five

The Complex
Mark and Travis

Mark made his way down the corridor, toward the room from which Travis was taken. He rounded a corner and ran right into his friend. Both men raised their handguns and quickly lowered them. The two of them were shaking their heads and then smiled.

"Let's go," Mark whispered.

Travis followed him down the hall while putting on the gear Mark handed him. They soon came to a door, which Mark opened, and both men entered into a room. They were in the observation room above the command center.

"Is that what I think it is?" asked Travis.

"Yep. The map of destroyed cities and countries, as far as I can tell," said Mark. "We need to take that room out so they can't launch those nukes."

"And how are we going to do that?"

"I have a few grenades in my pack," suggested Mark. "They will do wonders in the right areas."

"We need to evacuate that room first."

"That's your moral side talking, brother. Those people are the ones that will be responsible for a worldwide nuclear winter if we don't stop them. We need to take them and the computers out. This is war."

"You're right. Let's go stop this now."

They left the room and located the stairwell to get down to the command center. They both wanted to talk to each other about what had happened, but knew there would be time for that after they destroyed the room.

Once they reached the bottom of the stairs Mark stopped and removed four hand grenades from his pack. They devised a plan. Travis would take out the guards at the door and open it while Mark threw the grenades inside. The hope was that by destroying some equipment and the people who could make the launch of the ICBMs happen, it wouldn't.

Travis opened the door and they both moved into the hall. Travis took the lead and as soon as the guards were in view he shot them both with his handgun. The glass windows behind them shattered as the bullets hit after going through the men. The guards fell to the floor. Blood stains, like little red Rorschach test marks, were left on the wall below the window from the exit wounds, as they slumped to the floor.

They moved to the door just as an alarm started going off. Travis opened it and Mark pulled the pins on two grenades. While letting the spoons fly off, the distinct *ping* could be heard from each one, before he tossed them into the room. He pulled the pins on the other two and tossed them just as the first pair was exploding. The men took cover on the other side of the wall, while shrapnel ripped into the door and blew out the remaining windows. Shards of glass and concrete rubble rained down on them as they covered their heads. After the explosions blew the door off its hinges, they looked inside as the dust started to settle and could see the damage they made.

"I love the smell of composition B in the morning," commented Mark with a smile.

Travis just shook his head as they scanned the room. The internal alarm began to blast louder from speakers in the ceiling along the corridors.

Many of the computer monitors were destroyed and most of the people were down. The remaining screens were blank. A man, whose arm was severed above the elbow, was walking out of the black smoke. Blood was squirting out of the stump that was left, with pieces of flesh dangling. He was obviously in shock and was drooling blood while mumbling something that couldn't be understood. Mark took aim with his rifle and shot the man in the head to put him out of his misery. His lifeless body fell to the floor.

"That should do it," said Travis, "now let's get the hell out of here before we have company."

"Good idea."

He and Mark went back to the stairwell and started climbing to the surface. They knew the stairs only went up to Sub-level two, so they would have to find a way out from there. Using the elevator to get back up would be suicide, and they knew it.

When they reached Sub-level two, they were both out of breath after climbing so many stairs with all the gear and weapons they carried. While stopping to rest for a short time, Travis started to draw something in the dust on the floor.

"What is that?" asked Mark.

"I saw this on a lapel pin being worn by a guy who seemed like he was important. Do you know what it is?"

"I don't, but I've seen it before in Afghanistan, and that isn't good. We need to keep moving."

"I'm right behind you, brother."

"I think there's an access tunnel around here for vehicles," Mark pointed out. "While I was looking for you, I overheard some guys talking about the exhaust fans for carbon monoxide."

No one was roaming the halls after the alarm was sounded. Mark figured there must be a lockdown procedure everyone followed in case they were attacked. A map on the wall was located, showing a red dot where they were. Mark was right, there was a tunnel leading up to the surface.

"Let's go," said Travis, who took the lead.

Mark was right behind him as they proceeded up the passageway that they hoped led to the surface.

"What the hell were you thinking just walking in that room?" asked Mark.

"I was hoping they would just let me pass with my uniform on, looking all official-like," he replied.

"And how did that work out for you?"

Travis gave Mark a quick glare as he picked up his pace. Loud fan noises could be heard soon after they started walking.

"Exhaust fans," Mark announced, pointing overhead.

The tunnel was for bringing vehicles and supplies to the complex with the large concrete ramp moving down into the bowels of the Earth. They kept following it until it opened up into a large building on the surface and they could hear the alarm no more. The inside was full of aircrafts and vehicles. Only small windows allowed sun light into the room, so it was hard to make everything out. They skirted the room when suddenly all the lights in the building came on.

"What the..." Mark started to say, just as bullets started flying by them with whizzing sounds that meant they were too close for comfort.

"Down!" shouted Travis, pulling Mark behind an SUV just in time as bullets smacked the side of the vehicle where he had been standing.

As soon as they saw from where the enemy was shooting, Mark and Travis returned fire. Men in camouflaged combat gear and others in black BDUs seemed to be coming out of everywhere.

"Push right," Travis urged as loud as he could so that Mark could hear him over the gunfire.

Adrenaline was pumping through their veins and they seemed to be constantly re-loading fresh magazines into their weapons as the bad guys kept coming at them. The hangar was beginning to fill up with smoke from the burnt powder that all of the gun fire was producing, making it harder to see the targets until muzzles flashed. The sounds inside the large building were deafening as the battle raged on.

"Loading!" yelled Mark as he dropped another empty mag and put a full one into his M4. He had the new one inserted and was closing the bolt before the empty one hit the concrete floor.

Travis was soon yelling the same, and continued to alternate as men were dropping like flies all around them. They had been unscathed by flying bullets until Travis took one in his right shoulder.

"Ahhh!" he yelled as he moved to cover behind a steel beam running up the wall.

Mark saw him get shot, turned in the direction of the shooter and dropped him with three quick shots to the body, *thwack-thwack-thwack* was heard, then near silence soon after.

Everyone was low or out of ammo as the occasional click could be heard or just a few rounds were fired in their direction at a time. Travis's wound was superficial and he quickly got back into the fight after pouring a pouch of Quik Clot pellets on the wound.

"I'm out," said Mark.

"I have a few rounds left in my Glock," Travis replied, as he shoved the magazine back into it.

"How many are out there?" asked Mark.

"I see two guys making their way from the left."

"There's one behind that trailer, which makes three that we know of. I'm going for that gun right there, cover me," Mark said, pointing to his left.

He ran at the dead body as all three men started shooting. Travis stood up and dropped the two on the left. Mark ran and slid toward the handgun, hoping there was still ammo in it. He picked it up as he was still sliding on the slick concrete floor. He got the other guy in his sights, aiming at his head. Pulling the trigger, Mark felt the slide lock back on an empty chamber as the empty case and bullet left the gun. Unknowingly, the Sig 226 9-mm had one round left in it, which was enough to get the job done. The bullet hit the man just below his left eye and he fell back, splattering brain matter and blood on the wall behind him.

Mark got up and carefully made his way back to Travis.

"I think we got them all."

"Let's get the hell out of here!" Travis yelled.

They continued cautiously to the nearest outside exit and Travis opened the door.

He walked out into the fading light of the day on unsteady legs, while squinting.

Mark suddenly felt a warm spray coat his face, then he heard the sound of a firearm going off to his left. Travis's blood, he realized, as his companion fell back against the wall. Time screeched to a halt and everything went quiet for a split second..., then sounds of more gunfire could be heard, snapping Mark out of his momentary shock. He pulled his friend and brother back inside, slamming the heavy steel door with his foot.

Chapter Twenty-Six

The Hangar
Mark and Travis

"No!" echoed Mark, his voice bouncing off the walls throughout the large building.

Travis's lifeless body was lying on the concrete floor as Mark angrily smashed the window of an SUV next to them.

"Damn you all!"

Mark was overcome with grief, but knew he had to maintain his composure, because whoever killed Travis was still out there. Mark threw a couple of smoke grenades out the door to mask his escape as bullets hit against the building and door with loud smacking sounds. With a burst of adrenaline he almost effortlessly heaved Travis's limp body over his shoulder. They exited the building through the smoke screen and a hail of bullets. Mark recognized where they were when he moved past the edge of the smoke, so he made his way to the nearest truck, hoping it had keys in it.

He pulled open the back passenger door and laid Travis's body inside, then glanced up at the steering column. Luckily the keys were in the ignition, as was typical for most of the vehicles used by oilfield workers. He started it up, put the transmission into drive and pushed the accelerator to the floor. Gravel and dust were sent flying behind the truck as he sped out of the yard next to the airport. With no one in pursuit he headed to the control tower to get Christie and Schnell. He could hear bullets hitting the truck as he accelerated and figured they must be rounds from one or more snipers.

Mark knew he was in trouble now that he had lost his friend. Travis always had his back, and he could depend on him for anything.

After pulling up at the control tower next to the airstrip, he put the truck in park and hit the steering wheel a few times out of anger and frustration, the horn blared like his rage. He got out of the truck, slamming the door, then punched it over and over, denting it while bloodying his knuckles. Christie heard the commotion and ran out to investigate.

"What's wrong, and where's, Travis?"

Mark pointed to the back seat and walked inside the building. He heard Christie's sorrowful scream as the door shut behind him.

After a few minutes she walked in and it was obvious she had been crying the whole time she had been outside. Mark was sitting on a chair in the corner of the back room reflecting on everything that had happened the past few days. It had all been fast and furious since he left Afghanistan and he was very tired. The stim pill he had taken a few days ago was wearing off, he could feel it. His hands were shaking uncontrollably.

He had lost his only real friend in the world, a brother, and didn't know if anyone he knew was still alive besides Christie. His ex-wife Sara was out there somewhere, if she wasn't dead yet, but she had made her choice long ago. The death of their young son Michael wasn't his fault, but she still blamed him. It felt like a lifetime ago. He had recently stopped carrying a picture of him, as it was too much for Mark to handle. It was hard to focus on the job, any job, if he thought of his son. Michael had only been five years old when the tragedy happened. Mark was washing his truck in their driveway, while Michael was riding his bike on the sidewalk. A car came out of nowhere and the drunk driver jumped the curb hitting him. The police never found the man or the car. Soon after the funeral, Sara filed for divorce.

"Gotta keep going," he said to himself, as he got up, only to face another issue.

Whup-whup-whup noises could be heard from outside and Mark recognized them as helicopters. He told Christie to get down, out of sight of the windows. He went over to the weapons and ammo dump he and Travis had stashed in a closet and started to swap empty magazines from his dump pouch for loaded ones, filling his chest rig pouches. He was beyond tired, but had to keep going and fight for his life, Christie's and Schnell's. This wasn't the first time, and he knew it wouldn't be the last.

The helicopters flew over and the sound slowly went away. Mark finished loading his gear and weapons back into the truck and told Christie that they had to move.

"Where are we going to go?" she asked.

"Away from here so we can bury a hero and find a quiet place to rest."

The two of them and Schnell got in the truck and drove down the road as Mark carefully surveyed the area. Through eyes burning from the sting of sweat and held-back tears, he looked for a suitable place to bury his fallen brother.

Chapter Twenty-Seven

Kenai, Alaska
Alaska Militia forces and Army National Guard

The devastation to the small towns on the Kenai Peninsula was extensive. Buildings lay in heaps of rubble or on fire, or just smoldering. The streets were torn up from explosions, leaving craters all over, littering them with trash and parts of vehicles, houses and human remains. Not many things were moving on the streets. The army from Fort Richardson had done a good job repelling the Russian invaders alongside the locals, but the civilian population had taken heavy losses before the fighting subsided. Bodies were lying all over in the streets. There hadn't been time to collect any of them or even check to see if people were still alive. Enemy snipers were ruling most areas and made it hard to check on the wounded. The occasional dog was seen running by the perimeter security areas set up in different sections of town. Possibly running scared or looking for its owners.

"Sir," started a young soldier. "I'm getting a strange message on the coms."

"What is it?" asked the lieutenant, who had been in the fight since the beginning. The tall, lean young Army officer walked over to the radio operator and took the headset.

"I don't hear anything."

"Just wait, sir."

The voice came back on the radio, "This is Gen. Nathan Bailey commander of all remaining ground troops on the Kenai Peninsula....AAAHHHH!"

"That's it?" questioned the lieutenant.

"Yes, sir and it keeps playing over and over every few minutes."

"We need to round up all available troops and find the general. We need answers and he's our best bet. Call in all patrols and rally at the ball fields by the airport."

"Yes, sir," said the soldier.

Between the recorded burst from the general, the radio operator started calling in the patrols and outlying units.

As soon as everyone was ready, the small group got in a staggered column and moved out. They hoped they would link up with more than just a few people, but the lieutenant knew that the whole area had been devastated and didn't hold out much hope for many survivors.

On the way to the rally point they stopped to check for vitals on people who didn't look as bad as most others, but didn't find any survivors. The outcome of the conflict was looking grim for those who were still among the living. Shopping centers and food outlets lay in ruins. Medical supplies, food and water would only last so long. Alaska was isolated from the rest of the United States and most everything was trucked or shipped in.

The group consisted of civilians, Army National Guard and regular Army. The young lieutenant was the ranking officer, so they all took orders from him.

Chapter Twenty-Eight

Deadhorse, Alaska
Capt. Jackson, 25th Infantry Division

When the worn-out Army officer finally woke up, the first thing he did was look at his watch. He had been asleep for more than ten hours. He stood up quickly and kicked Burns boots. The old master sergeant got to his feet as fast as he could.

"Why the hell did you let me sleep?" Jackson asked.

"Sir, we all needed it, and I had men acquire trucks and supplies while on a watch rotation of the area. Here is the information you asked for. We are ready to head west just as soon as you give the order."

"I want all men bright eyed and bushy tailed in twenty minutes. Have them fed and in top shape. The fight I see coming is going to be a long hard one."

"Yes, sir," said Burns, who walked briskly away.

Jackson looked over the list of weapons, ammo and equipment. It wasn't much, but they would have to make do. Half of the list consisted of enemy weapons, rifles, machine guns and RPGs. Only the most seasoned soldiers would be using the AK-74s and other foreign weapons. This would allow for the younger troops to have more ammo for their M4 rifles. The other side of the list was an accurate count of all the men they had lost just from their unit, killed in action, wounded in action and the worst one missing in action. A separate list showed all of the men they had acquired along the way and their unit designations.

Once the captain was ready, he issued orders to platoon sergeants to get their men assembled by the vehicles and bring in the perimeter security.

Capt. Jackson walked toward the convoy and called for all the men to rally around him.

"Men, I know these past few days have been hard on all of us, but we must continue to fight if we are going to prevail against the enemy and win our country back."

Cheers were heard from the men.

Burns got the nod from the captain and yelled, "Mount up, ladies!"

With less than one hundred men left out of his entire company of 217 original combat troops, Jackson watched them load up in oilfield service trucks and start to drive away. He hopped in the last vehicle and joined the convoy as it headed west. With no scout vehicles, drones or satellites to access, they were on their own. The enemy could ambush them anytime and they would have the fight of their lives on their hands in an instant. With no idea of troop strength or location, they would most likely be ambushed along the road. The men were ready to fight, but it weighed heavily on Jackson's mind, along with the fate of his own family.

Chapter Twenty-Nine

Deadhorse, Alaska
Mark and Christie

After finding a small portion of a building that hadn't been completely destroyed, Mark and Christie stopped to rest for a while. They found a small room that was still in one piece. Mark locked the door and pushed a file cabinet up against it. Christie had been watching him closely, with a concerned look on her face as they got comfortable. She could see the pain in Mark's eyes as she moved closer to him.

He had taken most of his gear off and was just sitting there.

"Are you OK?" she asked Mark.

He looked up at her, then looked away again without saying a word. His thoughts were locked, like the slide on a Glock with a stovepipe jam.

"I know, that was the wrong thing to ask. Is there anything I can do? I feel like I've been pretty useless since I got shot and you have taken on every task by yourself."

Mark attempted to clear his dry throat and speak. "You've been a great help and inspiration on this whole fucked-up journey. I'm glad you're here, I've just got a lot on my mind. There's still something that doesn't add up about this whole thing."

Christie sat at the base of the chair he was in and hugged Mark's leg while laying her head on his lap. He stroked her hair which seemed to help calm him down. She looked up at him with loving blue eyes that seemed to speak to him. She had never looked at him like that before. He could see the emotion gleaming back at him between long lingering blinks. Her smile confirmed it.

After staring at him for a few moments, she said, "What?" in a soft, timid voice.

Mark pulled her close to him.

"Did I ever tell you I have a weakness for redheads?"

"Really?" she asked. "You never gave me any indication that you were interested in me. Not even the slightest hint."

"It's my military training, I guess. Never let the enemy know what you're thinking and never let your guard down."

"So, I'm the enemy?"

"In a manner of speaking... yes, you are. You're full of temptation and can render me helpless with very little effort."

Christie smiled, and then started laughing.

Mark stared at her with a confused look on his face.

"Why are you laughing?"

"Because that's the most ridiculous thing I've ever heard. If you were interested then you should've said something."

"I wanted to at first when you started renting from me, but I knew it was just a bad idea."

"Why would you think that? I might have said yes."

"That's precisely why I didn't ask," said Mark. "If we had started something I still would have left for months at a time or longer, and you would have moved out because our long-distance relationship wasn't working out. Then I wouldn't have had anyone to watch my dog or my house and besides, I'm old and used up."

"I see where you're coming from, but life is full of risks and you have to take them in order to live a little, and you're not old." she said beaming with obvious love in her eyes.

"Darlin', if you haven't noticed, I *am* a risk taker. There was this one time in Afghanistan..." Mark began, but what he was about to say was never heard. Christie had risen to her knees and met his lips with her own, cutting him off. Startled, Mark grabbed her by the shoulders and pushed her back. Her eyes slowly opened as her cheeks flushed with color.

"What's wrong?" she asked, slightly embarrassed.

"This isn't right," Mark said. "Too much is happening. We aren't thinking clearly. What I said before... I was just talking."

"Maybe we need to stop talking. Too much *is* happening, but we can help each other forget for a while."

Christie's eyes met his again, and now he knew he couldn't resist her. In one fluid movement he slid his hands down her legs and picked her up. She curled them around his waist as she pressed her body against him. Her lips found his as he opened his mouth, his tongue searching for hers. She pulled her mouth away, as if teasing him, and then kissed him forcefully when she heard his heavy breathing. He lowered her onto the floor, then unlaced and took off his boots. Her hands found his belt and then the buttons on his pants as he raised his hand behind his back and pulled his shirt over his head. She pulled his pants down as far as she could reach; he used his feet for the rest and kicked them off. Rolling on top of him, she slid down and took him into her mouth. Her tongue rolled over his tip and she could feel his body tense with pleasure. She rose up and smiled as she moved back up to kiss him again.

He ran his fingers through her hair and pressed the back of her head toward his, deepening their kiss. She could feel his heart pounding in his chest. She pulled back from him and stood up, slipping off her shoes and unbuttoning her pants. She slid them slowly down her legs and stepped out of them. Crossing her arms by the bottom of her shirt she pulled it up over her head, dropping it on top of the pile of clothes. She took off her bra as she lowered herself back down to the floor. Mark pulled her close and felt the soft skin of the small of her back underneath his rough, calloused hands. Rolling Christie underneath him, he spread her legs with his knees. His mouth closed around her left nipple as his fingers moved in and out of her. She moaned softly as she held his head to her breast. Her hips began to rock rhythmically in time with his fingers. Feeling her grow wet, his need became more urgent. Rolling his tongue over to her other nipple, he moved up to her mouth once more as he shifted his body higher to meet hers.

"I want you inside me," she moaned.

He pushed himself roughly inside her with one hand, pinching her nipple with the other. She cried out in a mixture of pleasure and pain. He reached between her legs and began to rub her as he moved with more urgency. He could feel each orgasm as they pulsed through her and took her breath away. As he felt her let go again, he followed, spilling inside of her. Breathing heavily, he withdrew from her and lay beside her on the floor. Too exhausted to speak and out of breath, she curled into him, intertwining her hand in his while wrapping her other arm around his side. For several minutes, their breathing filled the silence between them.

Christie slowly kissed his neck, then quivered.

"Wow, that was incredible. You're amazing!"

"Glad you liked it," said Mark, very matter-of-factly, with a smile showing his humorous side.

"How's your wound? I didn't even think about it until now."

"It hurts, but it will be OK," she said, as she started quivering again.

"Are you cold?" asked Mark as he sat up.

"No, I feel fine," she replied with a smile, and then lay back on top of him.

Mark covered them both with some clothes and enjoyed the closeness of being there with her, as they both fell asleep. Schnell had been guarding the door the whole time and stayed vigilant.

They awoke sometime the next morning to the sound of distant machine-gun fire, mixed in with other small-arms. No rounds could be heard hitting the building, so Mark was hopeful they were miles away. They quickly dressed, and Mark went around to all the windows, carefully looking out, but could see nothing of importance, then glanced at his watch.

"We need to move," he told her. "I know you're probably hungry like I am, but we need to find a safer place to be for now. If we can find a way, we should head south to the west side of Cook Inlet. I have friends down there and they should be out of harms way."

Chapter Thirty

Deadhorse, Alaska
Day 7
Mark, Christie and Schnell

They made their way over to a housing complex. Many of the exterior doors were open and windows were broken out. Once inside they carefully checked the rooms, looking for people and supplies, but found very little and no survivors. Schnell was in the lead with Mark trailing, Christie brought up the rear. He had shown her how to use his Beretta again and she carried it as they searched, with her index finger straight and off the trigger. The electricity and heat were still somehow on, making the rotting bodies stink in the parts of the building that had unbroken windows and closed doors.

Christie whispered in a muffled, voice covering her face, "It smells like a public bathroom that hasn't been cleaned in years, like an ammonia and fungus mixture... and poop."

"Rotting flesh will do that pretty quickly in the right conditions," replied Mark.

It wasn't strong enough to throw Schnell off the scent of explosives. She came across a trip wire running across the entrance leading into the dining hall. Mark looked back to tell Christie to stop, but saw her starting to enter a side room that he had only briefly looked in.

With no warning and total fury an explosive was detonated. Mark only registered a puff of pink mist to his left, but from his experience working around IEDs, he knew that in the split second it took him to realize what was happening, hundreds of tiny shards of shrapnel were ripping through Christie's soft flesh, sending her back out into the hall and slamming her against the wall with a sickening, wet *thud*.

Her right hand and both feet were gone. Just shreds of muscle, tendon and chips of bone were left protruding in their place. Bright red blood was squirting out of the stumps, pulsing in constant rhythm with her heart beat. Mark had been blown back by the concussion, and picked himself off the floor, his ears ringing. He hadn't been hit with any shrapnel, but was stunned. He could see the silhouette of a man with a rifle walk around the corner. He yelled, "Allahu Akbar," and Schnell attacked the man from the side.

The man shrieked in agony as Schnell sunk her teeth into his arm, causing him to drop his rifle to the floor. He backed down the hall trying to shake her off.

Mark shook his head and stumbled as he got up, but was able to focus quickly. He grabbed the man's rifle and pointed it in his direction.

"Vissza!" yelled Mark, and fired as Schnell moved back and out of the way. The man, his brown eyes wide open, dropped as Mark fired multiple rounds into him.

"Figyel," he said to his loyal companion, the command for guard.

She did as she was told and kept a watchful eye on the man, positioning herself between him and Mark and Christie.

Mark moved toward Christie and knelt beside her. He ripped a length of her shirt off and began making tourniquets to stop the bleeding from her arm and legs. She tried to speak, but only made a gurgling sound as she began to spit up blood. Her color was pale and her skin was beginning to look waxy. Her left eye was hanging from the socket.

A single tear fell from her right eye. Mark tried to console her. "You're going to be OK, baby!"

She started choking and gasping for breath.

"No!" yelled Mark as he saw the life leave her eyes and felt her body go limp.

He got up in a fit of rage started and kicking the lifeless soldier, then pulled out his Glock and shot him in the face. Schnell barked at him, as if telling him to stop. Mark called his companion over to him and she jumped up, putting her front paws on his chest, and then licked his face.

He instantly felt nauseous. A cold sweat started on his forehead as his cheeks flushed. His stomach churned as a small amount of stomach bile rocketed out of his mouth. He doubled over in pain as he emptied what little was in his gut. He slowly stood up, wiping his mouth, as Schnell whined, feeling his pain. His hands started shaking again like before, but this time they wouldn't stop.

"Man up!" he barked, almost wondering who said it. He seemed outside his body in the moment, detached. He took off his Barrett cap to wipe the sweat from his brow. Once again the hat was his lucky charm, as he was still alive, but he was starting to question if this was still a sign of good luck or was it a curse to always be the last man standing. Until he was sure, the cap went back on.

Mark looked again at the man who had killed Christie. He had darker skin and looked more Middle Eastern than Russian. He knelt down and went through his pockets and pouches, trying to find something that would help him make sense of everything. He opened a large pouch on his tactical vest and found an envelope with Arabic writing on it. The envelope had a ripped wax seal with the same insignia he saw during the briefing, before the mission to capture Umar Abdul just a few days ago. Inside was a short letter and a picture folded in half. He unfolded the picture, discovering that it was of him in Afghanistan the week prior, when he was meeting with Al Asari at the fueling station just north of Erazi.

"What the hell is going on?"

He had just killed the only person who could answer the many questions he now had. Mark put it all together quickly.

"You're a merc sent here to kill me?" he asked the dead man. "But why?"

Mark sat there quietly for a few minutes, trying to understand everything, before getting up and staring at Schnell. He put the picture back in the envelope, then put it in his pocket.

"Let's get out of here, girl."

She led the way out of the building as Mark followed, carrying Christie, wrapped in a table cloth from the dining hall.

He lay her down gently in the back seat, next to Travis. A couple of soldiers walked around the corner of a nearby building, pointing their rifles and yelling commands in Russian. Mark maneuvered to the front of the truck and let loose a thirty round magazine, blazing away wildly in their direction until the only sound he registered was the empty clinking of the last few brass shell casings hitting the gravel over ten feet away, as the bolt locked back. Once his rifle was empty he let it hang free in front of him, steam rising from the hot barrel. He then pulled his Glock out of his leg holster and emptied that mag into their lifeless bodies, as well. After spitting in their direction, he turned around and walked back to the truck. Before getting in, he loaded his weapons with fresh magazines.

Mark drove east to get away from everything, his grief most of all. Christie's death weighed heavily on his conscious, like a rucksack full of combat gear. He hoped that there were fewer things going on in the less-populated areas of the oilfield. After about ten miles he found what he was looking for. A construction site just off the main road appeared to have everything he would need.

He found a front-end loader with the keys still in it, which he started up and used to dig a grave for his friends. The ground was still frozen, so it wasn't the easiest task. He knew he was making a lot of noise, but this was the fastest way and he felt compelled to bury his companions.

I owe them that much, he thought.

Schnell was close-by, standing guard. The hole was almost done when she started barking and running in front of the loader to get Mark's attention. A few people were walking toward the area. He quickly shut off the loader and looked through his binoculars.

They didn't appear to be armed and looked like they had been run ragged. There were three men, with one trailing behind the front two.

He got out of the loader and slowly made his way toward the men. Schnell was slightly in front of him, as she always was.

When they got closer, Mark raised his rifle and commanded, "That's far enough! I want your hands up, turn around, get on your knees and put your right foot over your left!"

The overweight one of the group had to use his hand to move his foot and Mark scolded him for it. "Keep your hands up, chubby!"

He approached them and gave Schnell the guard command, "Figyel."

She maneuvered in front of them and growled, keeping them occupied while he came up behind and searched them.

After he was satisfied, he called Schnell over, backed away and said, "You men can get up and follow me."

"Who are you?" the man in a security uniform asked. "Are you Army or Marines?"

"Neither," replied Mark. "I'm just a civilian, like you... in the wrong place."

The men glanced at each other with confused looks on their faces, and then looked in horror as they saw what Mark had been doing.

"Qui C'est qu'a?" asked the short bald man.

"They're my friends and I was about to put them to rest."

"You know what he said?" asked the security guard. "He only talks like that when he's nervous or excited."

"I speak a little Cajun," Mark replied.

The men helped Mark pick up Travis and Christie and lay them in the grave side by side.

Mark thought Christie looked at peace now, almost asleep. He tried to imagine how she had looked before the last few days. He couldn't help but brush a lock of her hair over her injured eye. Marines weren't supposed to cry, but he allowed himself to shed tears for her and his fallen brother.

He knew that in the permafrost, even in the summertime, they would be well preserved. Mark told the men to move out of the way, then pushed the dirt and gravel back into the shallow grave with the loader, covering them up.

Mark just stared at the fresh grave for a while, and the other men waited for him. He closed his eyes, lost in a thousand memories from the distant past, and some from much more recently.

"Let's go," he finally said.

They all got in the truck and started down the road.

"Where can we find something to eat?" asked Mark. His grief still suppressed his appetite, but he knew he needed to keep his strength up with sustenance.

"We can go out toward Endicott Island," said the security guard. "There's a drilling rig on the way that has a camp beside it that may be untouched by what's happened."

"I doubt that, but it's worth a shot," said Mark. "How did you three escape the soldiers, anyway?"

"There were nine of us, if that tells you anything," said the tall thin man.

"Was it the Russian soldiers that killed the others?"

"I think so, but the other day we saw a group of them stop, take off all of their gear, lay down little mats and start praying like Muslims do at a mosque."

"Interesting," Mark responded.

"My name's Hank," said the short bald man after a pause in the talking. Mark could tell the scared man was just trying to spark some friendly conversation.

"I don't give a shit who any of you are or what your names are. You will all be dead soon and that's just the reality of it. I will do my best to keep you alive, but I will fail."

The guys all looked solemnly at one another, without saying another word.

They drove for many more miles in silence on the gravel road until they came to a crossroads and the man with the security guard jacket told Mark to take a right. The road was long, moving through the flat tundra, but after a short time the derrick of the rig came into view, as well as the camp and other small structures mixed in with the well houses.

"Looks like this place got hit pretty bad," said Mark, surveying the area.

It appeared that a few large blasts had destroyed the drilling rig and supply building, as twisted steel and cable was lying all around the pad. Some vehicles had burned to the ground, while others were bullet-hole ridden with most of the windows shot out. With the bodies scattered about the gravel, it was apparent to everyone that no quarter had been given.

"All of you need to be very careful as to where you go. We need to stick together and move slowly. Where can we find the mess hall?"

A finger from the back seat pointed toward a standalone building on the edge of a small lake, so that's where Mark took them. He parked a small distance out and told the men to stay in the truck. He and Schnell got out to recon the building. It had some large holes ripped in its outside walls from either grenades or RPGs. Some windows were shot out and black streaks covered parts of the walls where fires had been burning. She took the lead and carefully made her way up the stairs to the main door. He slowly opened the door and looked inside for trip wires. Schnell was sniffing the ground and walking carefully, with Mark close behind.

The inside of the structure smelled of death. After trying a light switch with no success, he concluded the power was off, so he used the weapon light on his rifle to brighten the dark corridors. The narrow beam brought many corpses into view, their skin parchment white. The odor of decay hit him like a slap to the face and he fought the urge to vomit. Mainly civilians were found along the way, but a few Russian soldiers were lying among the dead, as well.

The oilfield workers must have attempted to fight back and gotten lucky with a few, Mark thought.

After a thorough search, Mark went out to get the others. Upon exiting the building he immediately saw that two Russian soldiers had all three men on their knees in front of the truck. Judging from the position of their Kalashnikovs, they were about to execute them.

Schnell got their attention right away as Mark aimed down his sights, quickly dropping the first one with a center mass shot, and wounding the other as he fired two fast shots hitting his shoulder and the other struck his upper chest. Schnell ran up to the wounded soldier grabbing him by the arm. Mark ran over to them as the three men were getting out of the way. He started yelling at the man in Russian, which took the workers by surprise. Mark then pulled his Glock out of his leg holster and shot the soldier in the right leg, yelled at him some more, then shot him in the left leg. The soldier was screaming and pleading with Mark. After determining he would get no information, he fired one final shot at the Russian's head.

"I found some food" Mark said calmly to the three men, while holstering his sidearm. "Let's go get some, I'm starving."

The men were even more dumbstruck now than they had been before. They wanted to thank Mark for saving their lives, but didn't want to anger him, because they all agreed that he was unstable as he walked back inside the building.

"I don't know if we should trust this guy," admitted the man in the security clothing.

"What else are we going to do?" asked the Cajun. "We know he can handle himself and seems willing to help us."

"We should keep a close eye on him."

They followed him into the camp so they could get food and water.

The four men and Schnell ate their fill in the camp's kitchen and stuffed as many bags as they could find with non-perishable foods and water bottles. They were making their way to the front door when Schnell's ears perked up and Mark stopped them.

"Wait here," he said, walking over to the door, opening it slightly, looking out, then closing it. "We have a small squad of Russian soldiers outside. I need a distraction so I can eliminate them. You two go back to that side room with my dog, and you, Slim," he said to the security guard, "go to the window over there and start making noise to get their attention."

The men did as they were told, and as soon as the man by the window started making noise, the soldiers immediately maneuvered toward the door. Mark was ready as he whispered to himself, "These soldiers are about to have a bad day."

Mark positioned himself twenty feet down the hallway that made this area a perfect chokepoint. As soon as the soldiers barged through the door he started shooting from the kneeling position. Three of them fell right in the doorway, blocking it open, which worked right into Mark's plan. He quickly grabbed the flash-bang and grenade he had sitting beside him and moved to the door. He pulled the pin on the flash-bang and tossed it out, then pulled the pin on the grenade and threw it in the same direction. There was a loud noise and flash, followed by an explosion that rocked the front of the camp and sent out a shower of lead and broken glass from the windows. Mark called Schnell and they went out the front to finish them off.

Ping-ping, was heard as bullets hit the structure they were in. Shards of glass were flying everywhere as windows were being shattered.

"Ahhh...strelyat' v nego," yelled a Russian soldier standing close to the building, over and over until he finally fell silent as more gunfire was heard.

A few minutes later a silhouetted figure filled the door by the bodies of the dead Russian soldiers. "Let's go, boys," said Mark as Schnell appeared beside him.

Gasps could be heard coming from the three men, their eyes wide with fear.

"What was that guy saying out there?" asked one of the men.

"He was telling the others to shoot me," replied Mark.

As they exited the building, all they could hear was a constant, rhythmic pounding that turned out to be their own heart beats. As they followed Mark to the truck, none of them could believe what they saw outside.

Chapter Thirty-One

Deadhorse Airport
Mark and three oilfield workers

There were dead Russian soldiers strewn about, body parts and blood covering most of the pad in front of the camp. Some just had bullet wounds, while others had limbs missing or were just pools of goo. The copper smell of the blood was unavoidable for Mark and the men, as was the scent of explosive residue and burnt gunpowder that still lingered in the air. Shell casings and shrapnel littered the ground around them. The taller man in the group vomited at the sight, losing all that he had just eaten. He doubled over and went to vomit again, but not much came up from his now-empty stomach, except a small amount of bile. He wiped his mouth with the back of his dirty hand.

As soon as they all got in the truck, Mark started talking as if what had just happened was no big deal.

"Well, boys, what do you say we get the hell out of Dodge?"

"Sounds good," said the short bald man nervously, and the other two agreed, although one shook his head in disbelief.

Mark continued to do most of the talking, but together they devised a plan to get out of the area by plane. The other men chose their words carefully, since they were all scared of their newfound savior.

Mark discovered that the three men consisted of a security guard and two oilfield workers.

He didn't want to know their names, so he gave them nicknames. The short man from Louisiana was named Chubby, the man in the security guard coat was Slim, and the man who didn't speak was Sparky, because he was always fidgeting.

They agreed to help acquire a plane and fly with Mark in exchange for his continued protection. They drove to the airfield in Deadhorse to see if any aircrafts were still operational.

As they got closer the men couldn't believe their eyes as they focused on the destruction of the oilfield town. Many buildings had been destroyed by either explosions or fire. Vehicles were bullet-ridden much like they had seen in other areas. It wasn't long until they reached the airport.

Most of what they saw was destroyed, along with a large portion of the tarmac. The artillery barrage that Mark had been through the previous day had made gaping holes in the normally smooth, black runways. They decided to look in all the hangars along the way. They finally found a small ERA turbo prop on the side of one building.

"Will that one fly, son?" asked Chubby.

"It should," replied Mark.

They got out of the truck and approached the plane. Schnell got wind of something and pointed in the direction of another hangar. Mark couldn't provide security and check to see if the plane was worthy of flying. He asked Slim, the security guard, if he had any experience with weapons.

"I'm an Air Force veteran, that's how I got this job. So, yes, I can handle weapons pretty good," affirmed the tall man with a crew cut and thick black moustache.

Mark reluctantly gave him an AK-74 he had in the back of the truck and told him to keep an eye out, but not to shoot at just anything. "If it shoots at you, then shoot back," he told the man, who just nodded with a frightened look on his face.

Schnell kept looking in the direction of the next hangar over, so Mark told the man to watch that area specifically.

The others stood behind the truck and had the doors open for cover, just in case. Mark got in the cockpit of the plane and started flipping switches. The engine turned over and he could see that it had plenty of fuel. He taxied out from the hangar just as bullets started flying from one of the buildings on the right.

Slim started shooting back from behind the cover of the truck as a few soldiers advanced from a distance. It was unknown who they were, but it didn't matter. Mark was yelling for them to get in. As soon as the three men entered the ERA de Havilland Dash 8 small passenger plane, he asked if Schnell made it in yet. The men looked around and one of them said, "No."

Mark moved away from the hangar area to avoid the incoming small-arms fire and then saw his faithful companion running full speed to intercept the plane. She barely got aboard before Mark poured on the power and took off.

The door was closed as soon as she got into the cabin and he was finally able to take off. Looking over all the instruments as they gained altitude, Mark was optimistic that none of the bullets had damaged any vital systems.

"Where are we headed, son?" asked Chubby.

"We're headed to the *Sanctuary,* said Mark.

"The what?"

"We're heading for Fairbanks, to a small cabin I own that has a bunker under it with guns, ammo, medical supplies and food. I call it my *Sanctuary*. It's a home away from home."

Even though he had left the area and headed north to get away, Mark hoped that things back home had stabilized by now. The plan of going to Deadhorse didn't work out as well as he had thought it would. In fact, it had been a disaster. There was no way to have known that there would be a power struggle between the U.S. and Russia for the region.

The men settled in as the plane gained more altitude. The air was slightly choppy in the early evening sky. High cloud cover was moving in from the west and made everything less visible as darkness slowly enveloped the arctic. The horrible destruction was slowly left behind. Schnell moved to the cockpit and was nuzzling up to Mark and licking his hand.

"It's going to be OK girl," he promised as he stroked her head, showing her affection. "We're going to head south and go see James, Shelia and Andy."

She let out a bark that echoed in the confined space.

Mark knew that she loved the beach, and Andy for that matter. So far, everyone he knew had been taken from him. If they were still alive at the lodge, he had to get to them.

The flight was full of turbulence, but Mark didn't want to fly too high and be seen by any aircrafts. He didn't want to fly too low and be seen by anyone on the ground either. The clouds would temporarily camouflage their presence, but they would have to descend once they got closer to Fairbanks.

It took almost two hours to reach their destination, but they had plenty of fuel. The plane had a range of about a thousand miles fully loaded. They could fly much farther with only a few people on board.

Not long after passing the Brooks Range, the air smoothed out at the twelve thousand foot ceiling at which he was flying. The men in the back were sleeping now, which gave Mark time to reflect on the past few days. Despite the deaths of so many good men he had experienced in the past, the deaths of Christie and Travis were different. They weren't just companions in a war, they had been friends. He and Travis had seen each other through some terrible times and had come out the other side better friends because of it. He couldn't bear to open the thoughts of Christie. The relief felt by finally expressing what had always been in the back of his mind was crushed by the sorrow of losing her so quickly. Better to repress the feelings than try to deal with them now. There would always be time for that later, if he survived.

"It's just war," he mumbled to himself. "Nothing we can do about it."

No other planes could be seen on the radar the whole flight, even when they got close to Fairbanks. All was quiet. They passed down through the clouds and thick columns of smoke from different areas were rising from the ground. The thick plumes in the middle of the forest fires looked like volcanic eruptions.

"Forest fires," Mark yelled to his passengers.

Mark flew in a slow left bank around the smoldering city once it came into view. Pockets of small fires still flickered. He had dimmed the cabin lights and donned his night vision for the landing. Not much could be seen moving below. He circled around a few times, then flew out to the lake to check on the cabin before setting the plane down. The three men had unbuckled and were gazing out the windows while talking amongst themselves. Mark couldn't make out what they were saying because of the noise from the props.

After being satisfied that nothing would get in their way on the ground, Mark found a stretch of road close to the lake that didn't have any vehicles or debris on it, from what he could tell.

"Attention passengers, this is your pilot speaking, please put your seatbacks and tray tables in the upright and locked position and make sure your seatbelts are securely fastened. This could get interesting," he said on the intercom.

The men did what he said and braced for landing as they felt the plane descend rapidly.

Mark dove down and leveled out just before landing, like he would in a hot spot to avoid any small-arms fire. He knew that just because he couldn't see anyone didn't mean they weren't there.

After touching down he taxied to a small turnout to get the plane off the road as much as possible. Mark shut the engines off then opened the door, looking and listening for any signs of life. Schnell jumped out and started doing recon. The men filed out and Mark told them to watch the area while he disabled the plane. They didn't understand, but did as they were told.

Mark lifted the cover on the outside of the cockpit, removed a few items that they couldn't see and put them in his cargo pocket. He looked around the area and told the men to follow him.

When they reached the lake they stayed back in the tree line just enough so they wouldn't be seen. Schnell knew the area well and led them to the cabin a couple miles away. She stopped from time to time to listen or sniff the air, but kept going. Once she reached the edge of the alders on the east side she stopped and stared at the cabin until Mark caught up.

He took off his pack and removed a thermal imaging monocular from it. Starting from the far left he scanned to the right. Even slight heat signatures could be picked up, so Mark felt confident that everything was OK outside.

Skinny birch trees were scattered around the area with patches of alders closer to the lake. Mark hadn't maintained much of the area around the structure due to his being gone so much, and for the seclusion. Only a four-wheeler trail led to the cabin, snaking between the trees.

"Now to see if we have any company," he whispered to Schnell.

The faithful German shepherd methodically made her way to the cabin and walked around it before stopping near the stairs up front, signaling to Mark she was satisfied.

The four men slowly approached the structure with Mark, "The Protector" as he was now being called by the others, in the lead.

The lock was still on the front door and all the windows were intact. He couldn't believe it, but this would mean no one would be inside. Mark entered the combo on the lock. He then opened the wooden door, revealing a steel door directly behind it. The other men looked at each other in amazement as they waited for this one to be opened, too. After opening a side panel and placing his thumb on a pad, the door opened for Mark. They all walked in and the lights automatically came on.

"This is one high-tech place," Slim observed.

"There are fresh towels in the bathroom," said Mark. "Food in the cabinets, but it has to be cooked, because it's all freeze-dried. If you have a question about anything in here, that means you shouldn't touch it without asking me first."

The men agreed with Mark and took turns showering. Fresh clothes were given to them, but most of them didn't fit so they just put on their old, dirty ones. They ate a meal made from freeze dried food that had been cooked on the propane stove. The taste of the beef stroganoff made some of their noses turn up, but it was food and they knew it would keep them alive and were glad to have it before settling in for the night.

Mark explained that they were welcome to stay with him as long as they wanted.

"I've got several years worth of supplies in this little fortress," he told them. "But we will eventually need to venture out and get vital information and other supplies."

Mark turned on the radio and flipped through the channels, trying to find someone out there talking, as they all sat down and relaxed. Nothing but static was found on the FM band, so he flipped over to the AM side. After going through the stations two times, he went back to 97.4 because of the break he kept hearing in the static.

"I need to try and boost the signal," Mark said.

After running some wires from his antenna on the roof to the radio, the static slowly turned to a slow recording that could barely be made out.

"Did that say there's a *safe zone* in Canada?" asked Chubby.

"Could be a trick," Slim volunteered.

"We can try to find out more information tomorrow," said Mark. "I know of a radio tower not far from here, if it's still standing."

They thanked him for his hospitality and one by one crawled into sleeping bags Mark had rolled out on the floor for them to get some much-needed rest. Mark retired to his own room.

"We need to keep an eye on them girl," Mark whispered to Schnell as they sat in his room finishing cleaning weapons. "I'm going to take a shower and clean my wounds. Tomorrow, you can have a bath." She whined a little when she heard bath, but she would be good for her master, as she always was.

The night was uneventful and the morning was a late one for most in the cabin, as they slept in. Mark was up early. A nightmare woke him. It was about Christie's death and was as vivid as it was when it had happened. He remembered the reoccurring one he used to have about his son Michael. Most mornings he would wake in a cold sweat, his sheets soaked like a canteen spilled all over as he slept. As soon as he realized where he was, he got up and cooked scrambled eggs out of a can after a quick recon of the surrounding area. He then took Schnell into the bathtub for a well-needed cleansing, like it was business as usual.

When she was done she ran around the main room, shaking and rolling on her back all over the floor, to dry off. Her tongue was flopping as she did all this and Mark could tell she was happy.

After about ten minutes she suddenly stopped and listened intently. The men stopped laughing and talking as they started to feel the vibration, too.

"Something, large like a tank or another tracked vehicle, is in the area," Mark told them. "Get ready to move if we need to."

He went to his room and put on his tactical vest and weapons, while the others put on their boots and coats.

Mark opened a laptop sitting on the desk by the front door. After the screen came to life and he entered a password he could see six video camera feeds. The others stayed back, but looked on intently to see what might be coming for them.

"Yep, we have company, boys." Mark moved out of the way so they could all see what was on the screen.

Chapter Thirty-Two

Fairbanks, Alaska
Day 7
Mark, Chubby, Slim and Sparky

The column of T-90 tanks with 125-mm main guns and BTR-80 eight-wheeled amphibious, armored personnel carriers with 30-mm guns, were definitely not American. They were caught on video while they passed by camera number four that was set up by the highway. Dozens of troops were flanking most of the vehicles and some were riding atop the tanks. They were traveling on the same road on which Mark had landed the plane, tearing up the asphalt and dirt on the sides. Mark hoped they wouldn't destroy the aircraft, or he and the men would have to find another one that was worthy of flying.

The fact that the Russians were in Fairbanks in such great numbers was starting to reinforce to him and the small group the belief that America was losing, and fast.

"If they start checking the cabins on the lake, then we're in trouble," said Mark. "I didn't put a toilet in the bunker down below. It's strictly for storage or hiding, not long term survival. We can put up one hell of a fight with what I have in there, but with all the firepower they have, we won't last too long."

Mark went down below into the darkness and soon turned on a light. The security guard peered down the stairs and his face lit up, like a kid in a candy store.

"What's down there?" the Cajun asked.

"Guns, ammo, and totes with who knows what in them, likely more guns and ammo."

Mark told them to get back, and after a few minutes he started handing the men weapons and ammo. He had two squad-automatic machine-guns chambered in 5.56x45 with two hundred-round belts in cans below them, and extra cans. When he got the arsenal laid out on the floor, the other three were impressed.

"What are these little guys here?" asked Chubby.

"Those are flash-bang grenades used to stun," replied Mark, "and these are fragmentation grenades with a 15- meter kill radius. You can toss a flash-bang into a group of soldiers or a room and disorient them and either follow it with a frag or just shoot them. Throwing the frag and ducking behind cover usually allows you to not get shot or blown up and stay in the fight."

"What are these?" asked Slim.

"Those are M18A1 anti-personnel claymore mines. They fire about seven hundred tiny steel balls a distance of approximately one hundred yards with clear line of sight. They will destroy brush and trees that are directly in front of them. The shape charge keeps the blast contained to a smaller area."

"Front toward enemy," read Chubby slowly in his thick accent.

"I'll be putting these out as soon as it looks like it's safe to do so," Mark informed them.

The rest of the gear, weapons and explosives were explained to them all a few times. Mark had been to other countries and trained rebel soldiers that could barely speak English, or none at all, so this was a cakewalk for him.

Radios and throat mics were handed out and instructions were given on operating these, as well. They looked in depth at a map of the area. Places that were marked in blue were safe places that Mark had dug out or built up in order to defend, if needed, and displace if necessary.

"What do you mean, displace?" questioned Chubby.

"It means to fall back," said the other man that had barely spoken the whole time.

"Well hello there, Sparky," Mark smirked. "You finally ready to join us with our plan to repel the enemy at all costs?"

"I'm ready to get the hell out of here and go home."

"Listen, Carl," said Slim, the security guard. "We all want to go home, but we need to fight to survive or there won't be a home for any of us."

"What did I tell you boys?" questioned Mark. "I don't want to know who any of you are, your names or anything. It's easier that way. Now, I need you on the monitor and keep in radio contact while I put these claymore mines out. If I need you guys, it will be in a hurry if the shit hits the fan, so be ready."

With six mines in hand Mark took one last look at the monitors then he and Schnell went out to strategically place them. He knew that after the armored column went by the lake they could have patrols being sent out to take care of anyone who might still be in the vicinity. When an army invades enemy territory they have two options, exterminate the populace or use them to their advantage in any and every way. The only way for the Russians to keep Alaska was to exterminate the populace, at least that's what he was gathering from the situation so far.

No resistance was met while Mark was setting the mines on trails and the shooting lanes he had made by clear-cutting the brush and trees. He knew that, like animals, the enemy would take the easiest route to advance on their objective. With the help of the men in the cabin watching the camera monitors, he was able to get the job done faster. He used remote detonators in place of trip wires to alleviate the fear that an animal might set one off.

The rest of the day was very quiet. Mark had been expecting something to happen, and just after 0500 the next morning, it finally did.

Throughout the night the men had taken turns watching the monitor. Mark was awakened when a few soldiers had been seen on camera two approaching the cabin.

Mark got dressed and attached a silencer to his M4 rifle and fastened a brass catcher to the side of it too. If he could take them out without making too much noise, they should be okay for awhile longer.

After he was ready he walked out the door and moved to intercept. Just as soon as they came into view he stopped and knelt by a tree with bushes in front. When the men got within fifteen feet he opened fire, dropping them all. He decided to carefully reposition them to face the lake, like they had been shot by a sniper across the way. He knew this would fool the standard foot soldier, but not a trained spec-ops warrior.

After checking in with the over-watch in the cabin, he made his way back along the small trail.

Activity increased from all directions that day. Mark figured they must be looking for the lost patrol. There was no telling what they would do once they found them.

After dark the cameras were swapped once again to their green, fuzzy night-vision mode, and the men continued to watch the monitors. Patrols could be seen sweeping the area closer to the cabin.

"I think it's time we hit them hard," said Mark. "If they hit us in here, we're dead for sure. At least out there, we have a fighting chance."

The others didn't want to leave the cabin but agreed with the logic. They weren't trained like Mark, but they had the firepower to fight back to the best of their ability now. He knew that more instruction on the weapons would have been preferred, but there simply wasn't time for it.

All their gear and weapons were checked by Mark while the men asked some last-minute questions. Once they were done gearing up, they left. Slipping out of the cabin under the cover of darkness, each wearing a night-vision monocular, they made their way to their designated places. They split up into teams of two so they could cover each other while they reloaded. Each team had a machine-gun so they had fire superiority.

It was an uneventful night as the men waited for the inevitable. As the light of day was just starting to be seen on the horizon Mark spotted a patrol of five men approaching from the west of his position.

"Slim, Sparky," he radioed the other team to get ready for contact, but received no response.

"Those jackasses must have fallen asleep," he said to Chubby, who just shook his head. "Here we go," Mark announced, as he detonated a claymore with a *ka-BOOM* just in front of the small patrol.

The soldiers were caught off guard by the full force of the blast that illuminated the darkness, like the sun itself had exploded. The enemy was hit with the whole force of the explosion. All of them were either killed instantly or wounded very badly.

"What now?" said Mark's new partner.

"We wait."

The radio came to life in their ears, "What the hell was that?" said Slim's voice suddenly.

"I'm glad you boys are awake now," replied Mark. "I just detonated one of the mines and took out five soldiers. You boys stay alert over there and Slim, don't engage until they're almost on top of you."

"Do you think they're coming?" Sparky whispered.

"You can count on it," Mark replied.

Not ten minutes later the woods were swarming with Russian soldiers. They were making enough noise to wake the dead. The *whup-whup-whup* of helicopters flying search patterns could be heard all around them.

Pop-pop-pop, then small *burping* noises from automatic weapons mixed with explosions, could be heard in the direction of the other team. Mark just kept listening for the SAW and the M4 as the battle intensified. Their distinct sounds could be identified, mixed in with the rest of the Russian weapons. Soon after he and his new buddy were in a fight of their own. Mark heard the bang of frag grenades going off, shrapnel tearing through the trees and brush nearby. He threw a few of his own to stop advancing troops.

"Fire small bursts and choose your targets wisely," Mark yelled to his companion as they continued throwing hot lead toward the enemy.

Every time the SAW next to him ran dry he swapped Chubby his M4 while he quickly reloaded it for him.

"Keep firing small bursts in that direction, I'm going to flank them. Just *don't* shoot me."

The Louisianan did as he was commanded as Mark moved away. Mark hoped the gun would run empty by the time he got to the soldiers' position so he wouldn't get caught in the crossfire, and that's exactly what happened. The SAW stopped firing and the Russians got up to advance. There was about ten of them left, so Mark threw over two flash bangs and started shooting while moving forward on their right flank. He was able to take them by surprise and destroy their ranks. Some soldiers got lucky and fled before Mark could engage them. Others got away wounded, but he killed most of them.

He made his way back to his original position only to find his new cohort shot in the head by one bullet. He hadn't run out of ammo, he had been killed. Mark picked up the SAW, reloaded it, then moved in the direction of the other team. Once he got close he could see Russian soldiers standing over a single body. Without hesitation he started to mow them down with the machine-gun. Once the weapon was empty he lowered it and surveyed the immediate vicinity for any other threats.

Sparky, had been shot multiple times. There was still steam rising from the fresh bullet holes in his torso, crimson blood mixed with the dirt around him. His eyes were still open, like they were pinned in place, so Mark attempted to close them but they popped back open as if they were spring loaded. He looked around for Slim the security guard, but he was nowhere to be seen.

Mark heard a branch break to his right and quickly took a knee while bringing the weapon to his shoulder.

It was Slim walking toward him. "What the hell happened?" Mark asked him.

"They were everywhere and I fell back when my rifle jammed. I thought he was behind me," he replied, looking down at Sparky's lifeless body.

"We'd better get back to the cabin and get out of Dodge."

"Right behind you," said Slim.

Mark turned and took a step forward, then heard the *click* of a handgun hammer and stopped. He turned slowly to see Slim pointing his sidearm at him.

"What's going on here?" Mark asked the tall man.

"You have a bounty on your head, mate, and I'm the bloke who's bloody well going to collect it," Slim replied in a very strong English accent.

"I have to admit, I thought Sparky there was the dodgy one."

"Well, you can't always be right, now can you?"

Mark stepped toward Slim and the man grabbed the pistol with both hands.

"That's far enough."

"How much is the bounty, and is it dead or alive?" Mark questioned.

"Either way it's the same, $2-million U.S., but you would be easier to deliver alive, so go on, drop your weapons and gear and let's get on with it."

He did as he was commanded and slowly dropped his weapons. A noise was heard to Slim's rear, and as he turned to look Mark grabbed a knife from behind his back and threw it at the man. Slim turned back from seeing a squirrel just in time to receive the blade in his neck. He stood there for a few seconds in disbelief and then shot once, hitting Mark in his Kevlar body armor.

The man fell to one knee as Mark moved forward to finish the job. Mark kicked the gun from his hand and grabbed the knife, twisting and ripping it out of his throat. Blood sprayed from his carotid artery and only gurgling noises could be heard as Slim fell the rest of the way to the ground.

Mark watched as he bled out, then went to recover his weapons while his mind reeled about the bounty and the mercenaries that were sent after him for a reason still unknown to him.

He felt obligated to bury Sparky and Chubby, but didn't have the time, knowing the Russians would be back with an even larger force sooner, rather than later. He reloaded and moved back to the cabin to get Schnell. On his way there, he came into contact with more troops and dispatched them like the seasoned combat veteran he was.

Once he reached the cabin he carefully looked for any signs of an ambush. Satisfied there wasn't one, he entered and got as much gear, food and ammo together as he could carry. He and Schnell would hopefully be able to make their way to the plane he left by the road a few miles away and get up in the air before being seen.

His faithful companion could smell and hear the enemy before they could be seen by Mark, making it that much easier for him to take them all out within an instant, of them coming into his sights. He estimated that they had taken out more than fifty enemy combatants since first light. He hoped to hell that the plane was still in one piece.

As the road came into view he could see an intact ERA plane and felt better. He would need just a few minutes to put the small parts back in that he had removed, and get turned around for takeoff. Schnell would have to stay alert and warn him if someone was coming.

Once the plane was started and pointing in the right direction Mark throttled up with full flaps and was airborne almost instantly. As the aircraft climbed in elevation he saw something on the radar and began looking out the windows for confirmation.

Whatever it was it was climbing and heading almost straight for them. He kept looking at the radar as the object was getting increasingly closer to them. He continued to climb, leveling out around ten thousand feet.

Without any warning green tracers started flying by the turbo-prop, a few rounds hitting the plane causing it to shudder. Mark banked hard left to avoid the bullets that he could now see were coming from a Ka-50 Black Shark Russian attack helicopter. The aircraft was highly maneuverable. Mark knew going up against the military-grade helo with a prop plane designed for the public sector was like a shark pursuing a minnow. That knowledge combined with all the flashing lights and warning alarms going off in front of him made him wonder if this was the end of their journey.

"Hang on, girl," he told Schnell as he sped up and dove to try and outrun the attacker. Schnell was whining as Mark felt his stomach in his throat with the G- forces pushing hard against him. He knew the helicopter couldn't fly as fast as him in a dive, so he poured on the throttle and before reaching three thousand feet leveled off and flew as fast and straight as he could before climbing again. On the way back up his ears popped several times and Schnell began whining again.

"Almost done, girl," he told her.

The service ceiling of the enemy aircraft was only eighteen thousand feet, so if he could exceed that without needing oxygen himself, he was safe.

His plan was working and the blip on the radar was moving farther and farther away.

"See," he blurted out, "they gave up, and we're home free as long as fixed-wing aircrafts aren't called in to intercept us. We wouldn't stand a chance if that happened."

The rest of the flight south was uneventful, except for a little turbulence, until he noticed they were running low on fuel. Luckily they were close to Anchorage, and he hoped they could re-fuel there.

That was the idea until he came out of the mountains and the city came into view. He shook his head in disbelief at what he saw below.

Chapter Thirty-Three

South central Alaska
Mark and Schnell

Mark flew over the smoldering and war-torn city of Anchorage. From what he could see there was no one moving below. Much of the city was in ruins. Tall buildings were diminished to rubble. City streets were scarred with craters from artillery, air-to-ground missiles and bombs. Fires were burning in many areas of the large city, and black-and-gray smoke rose from other parts. Fortunately, the enemy was nowhere to be seen.

He found a small section of undamaged airstrip where he was able to land the plane at Ted Stevens International Airport, near the coast, in Anchorage. He flew around two times to try and draw anyone out, but saw no movement and decided it was safe enough to land. As soon as the wheels touched down on the tarmac he taxied around until he saw an avgas truck that looked like it was still in one piece. After stopping next to it he shut the engine down, looking around the area one last time before stepping out of the aircraft.

"Don't you go running off," he ordered Schnell before opening the door on the front side of the plane.

She jumped out and immediately found a place to relieve herself. She then started to scout the area. Mark wasted no time pulling the hose off the truck after looking at the sight glass level for the tank. The electric pump was down. Since there were no keys inside the cab to start the truck he began manually pumping the fuel with a small hand crank. It would take longer but it had to be done. After getting only 520 gallons into the tank of the aircraft, Schnell started growling in the direction of the terminal. Mark swapped hands on the pump and was able to transfer 70 more gallons before her growling got to an uncomfortable level. The tanks on the aircraft weren't completely full but he didn't know how far they would have to fly, either, so more was better. He laid the nozzle on the deck, capped the tank, backed away and he and Schnell slowly got in the plane. He started the plane, using only familiarization with the buttons and levers, while keeping an eye on the terminal and the rest of the immediate area. It started right away. Mark throttled up and pushed the flaps down. There was no time to taxi so he just poured on the power and was soon in the air. With no other aircraft in sight he didn't need to be on the main strip.

"What was out there, girl?" Mark asked his companion while patting her head.

Schnell barked, then put her paw on Mark's right hand while it was on the throttle.

The two of them flew southwest toward the homestead of the Isaaks' He hoped they had been out of the line of fire where they were on the west side of Cook Inlet.

They gained altitude, but not too much. Being a little lower he could see more of the area.

Mark and Schnell were soon flying over the oil and gas platforms in the water below. Some of them were burned and others were just vacant of any movement.

Boats of different sizes were adrift in different places, like a ship graveyard in the dark, gloomy waters below. Smoke was rising from the Kenai Peninsula and the Alaska Peninsula on each side of the inlet.

Once they got closer he decided to fly over the town of Kenai to see if anything or anyone had survived before heading to the west side.

Many buildings were destroyed and or still burning, similar to Anchorage. The bombardment that had more than likely come from the sea and air had taken its toll on the whole area. Entire sub-divisions had been wiped out, and not many structures remained completely intact. Burned vehicles littered the side roads and the highway. Small civilian aircrafts as well as military ones were heaps of twisted steel scattered across fields and roads. He was sure that the locals had put up one hell of a fight. Most Alaskans were well known for liking guns. He even knew of a statewide machine-gun association that more than likely helped defend the state from the invaders.

Mark banked right after flying around for a few minutes surveying the destruction and headed for the Isaaks' on the other side of Cook Inlet. It wouldn't take long to get there in the plane he was using.

Some smoke was rising above the trees on the north end of Kalgin Island, a small stretch of land in the middle of Cook Inlet. It covered approximately 22 square miles. The smoke and a few boats caught his attention as he went by. They were anchored just off the beach near the campfire.

"Looks like someone got away," he said to Schnell as they flew over.

Fifteen minutes later he slowed the airspeed down to a minimum as the beach came into view. Mark flew low and slow to evaluate the situation presented in front of him. Many black and brown bears could be seen feasting on something near the landing stretch of sand that James always used. Blood trails could be seen in all directions. The small planes owned by the Isaaks' and others along the beach were now burned heaps riddled with bullet holes.

Making another slow pass Mark decided to scare the bears away from whatever they were feasting on so he could land the large plane.

He opened the window on the left side of the cockpit, pulled the pins and dropped two fragmentation grenades. They hit the sand close to the bears and exploded about ten feet apart. Sand was blown several feet into the air and the bruins immediately scattered away at the sound and vibration of the explosives.

He circled back again and followed the direction of the wind sock. The landing was a bit rough in the larger plane, but he was able to handle it. After coming to a stop Mark and his trusted canine got out to investigate what the scavengers were doing.

As they got closer it became apparent that the bears had been eating human bodies. They were mutilated. "Only DNA would be able to distinguish who they had been," Mark said to himself.

A ripped-up, bloodstained green jacket with an NRA emblem on the back was found nearby, and Mark recognized it as James Isaak's. The man had worn that particular coat every time he had seen him in the past.

The hunting and fishing trips and visits were flooding his mind with the memories of the family. There was no wondering now. Their residence, along with the rest of the small community, had been rounded up and executed, just like so many others.

"We can't leave them here for the bears," Mark told Schnell as she walked back over to him after investigating for herself.

Mark walked down the beach to get a neighbor's tractor in order to dig a hole and bury what was left of his friends and their neighbors.

The tractor started right up, luckily, and as he was driving it down the beach Schnell barked as a few bears began coming back to get more grub. Mark stopped, put it in neutral and started shooting warning shots at the bears with his M4. He knew that the small caliber would only make them angry if he shot them, but he had to keep them away and hope they didn't dig up the remains later. With the noise and the rounds hitting close to them, the large animals scattered. Schnell kept her distance from the area to which the bears had fled and stayed by the tractor as Mark worked.

He dug the hole as deep as the bucket would allow, and pushed all the remains in before filling it back up with dirt. The process was time consuming with the small machine, but it got the job done.

After parking it on the mass grave he and Schnell walked up to the lodge to rest for the night and find something to eat.

Once they reached the building he could see that all the doors were shut, which was a good sign that no animals would be inside. But, it didn't rule out people being there. A thorough inspection of all the rooms answered that question. The electricity was off, so they went to the generator building to see what could be done to get it back on.

"Looks like it just ran out of fuel," he said to Schnell. Mark took the cap off the generator and began to pump fuel into it from a nearby drum. After topping it off he primed it and started cranking. He knew if he used the electric start the battery could die and cause a whole new set of issues. The contraption finally started coughing and then started, filling the room with black smoke. When they walked out they could see the whole lodge and all the out-buildings' lights coming on.

"Let's go turn all those lights off before they're seen by the wrong person," he said to his companion.

After making sure no one could tell they were there Mark prepared a hearty meal of canned moose meat and potatoes. The lights in the lodge were kept dim and blinds were closed for that very reason. He shared the satisfying meal with Schnell, then they both relaxed for a while on the love seats in the living room. He knew he needed a shower but didn't want to take a chance and regret it if someone came into the house.

He went upstairs and decided to use the room that had a view of the beach so he could keep an eye on the plane. Mark placed a dresser in front of the bedroom door as a hasty barrier, just in case someone tried to come in while he was sleeping. Schnell would warn him, but this would slow them down so he would have more time to react. He pulled the tactical harness off her and she shook, then rubbed her body on the carpet. She didn't mind wearing it, but was glad to have the equipment off.

Chapter Thirty-Four

Lake Clark National Park, Alaska
Alaska Homestead Lodge
Day 8
Mark and Schnell

The next morning, Mark got up, made coffee and was preparing to make breakfast in the kitchen when he began to wonder where the best place would be to hide out of harm's way. That's when he remembered the hunting cabin in the mountains nearby.

Suddenly Mark looked at his companion with excitement, causing her ears to perk up. "I know where to go," he said to her.

The two walked out the back and headed northwest to the log building from which he and Andy had hunted many times. If James didn't make it, maybe he sent Shelia and Andy away so they would be safe, or maybe they all were up out there. That still didn't explain James' jacket on the beach, though.

Being mainly uphill the walk was a slow one, but once on the ridge it got easier. Nothing was encountered on the way to the cabin and Schnell only stopped three times to listen, but, once satisfied everything was OK, she continued on. Mark took this as a good sign.

Soon the small cabin was in view, and just as he was about to call out to see if anyone was in it a bullet was fired at him. It ricocheted off a nearby tree and

Mark was pelted with splinters and bark as he hid behind another.

"It's Mark, stop shooting!" he yelled, hoping the shooter was James, Andy or Shelia.

The door slowly opened and out came a dirty Andy, barely able to walk. "Mark, is that really you?" he countered in a weak voice. He appeared to have been wearing the same clothes for a week, and they hung loosely from his body, which was much thinner than the last time Mark had seen him. He looked dehydrated and hungry.

"It's me, and Schnell, too. Are you alone?"

Andy sat down in the dirt, dropped the rifle and started crying as Mark approached, scanning the area with his rifle ready. Schnell had already made it to him and was licking his face.

"If you're here, and my parents aren't with you, then what happened to them?"

"I'm not quite sure, but I did find your dad's jacket on the beach and it didn't look good. Let's get back to the lodge, make you something to eat and get you cleaned up."

As he helped the boy to his feet Andy wrapped his arms around him, generating the biggest hug he could muster, while beginning to weep once more. Mark hugged him back and neither of them let go right away.

There was solace in finding one friendly, living face after all the loss and death he had encountered over the last few days.

"Are you crying, Mark?" Andy asked after he let go.

"I have something in my eye. It'll be fine."

"How did you and Schnell get here?"

"I'll tell you *all* about it on the way back, buddy," he said, mustering a smile.

Mark helped support Andy on the way back to the lodge, with Schnell running point. They talked on the way. He explained that Deadhorse hadn't worked out the way he planned, and the rest of the state he had seen so far was destroyed. He told Andy about the radio broadcast he had heard, so they decided Canada was where they should go.

Once back at the lodge Andy took a shower while Mark cooked them some food. The place was fully stocked for the upcoming tourist season so there was plenty to choose from. Some perishables had gone bad while the electricity was off, but eggs, hotcakes and sausage were readily available.

The grease from the sausage filled Mark's nose with the aroma of sage and pepper as it cooked.

"It smells good," commented Andy as he entered the kitchen.

Schnell stood patiently by the table and joined them in the feast after it was ready.

Andy had trouble focusing on eating. He kept stopping and staring at the wall to his left.

"You OK over there?"

The boy just nodded his head after Mark got his attention.

Mark knew that this couldn't be easy on him, having experienced such losses, himself. Finding Andy alive rejuvenated Mark's spirits and his will to go on. With Christie gone, Andy was the closest thing to family Mark had now, and he would keep him safe at all costs. If this *"Safe Zone"* really existed, then Mark had to get Andy there so they could begin some kind of life anew.

They finished breakfast a little later, then turned off the generator and grabbed as much food as possible. They were soon on their way to the plane.

Andy stopped near the grave that Mark had dug, and lingered for a bit.

"I saw it happen..." Andy blurted, almost choking on his words.

"You saw who that did this?" Mark asked.

"I saw them bring everyone down here, and they disappeared behind the cliff. From where I was on the ridge all I could see were the men shooting, but I could hear the screams above the gunfire."

"What did they look like?"

Andy went silent and Mark didn't press. He knew the boy would talk in his own time and he would be there for him.

"We should get going," Mark told him once everything was loaded.

The plane had a harder time taking off than it did landing, but with no load of people or cargo it finally got off the sand. They were starting to gain altitude when he turned to Schnell and told her where they were going. "How does Canada sound, girl?"

She barked her approval and the plane banked left and leveled out on a heading to the east.

Canada had always been neutral in wars, and after hearing the looped recording on the radio, it was a good bet that it might really be the right place to go. His training told him it could be a trap to lure people in, but that was a chance Mark was willing to take. He hoped that they would be safer there from a nuclear conflict than many other places. If the people in Deadhorse did get the system operational again it really wouldn't matter where on Earth they were, but a place away from ground zero would give them a fighting chance, at least for a little while.

They flew east toward Prince William Sound on a heading that would take them over the Chugach and Wrangell mountains and into the Yukon Territory. Mark knew they wouldn't get as far as he wanted with the limited amount of fuel on board, but they would go as far as possible.

Andy had fallen asleep with Schnell by his side shortly after take-off. It still wasn't clear to Mark what had happened to the Isaaks', but he knew that when the young man was ready, he would talk.

After many hours of flying the fuel gauge was pointing the wrong direction. Mark looked at the navigational computer for an airport. One was located at a place on the Alaska coast called Icy Bay. He had never heard of it but hoped they had fuel available.

He had flown through most of the night while Andy slept. Pink and yellow were finally seen on the horizon as a new day dawned.

They were a few miles away when the right engine sputtered and cut out. At almost thirteen thousand feet, Mark knew he had enough altitude to glide the aircraft in and perform a belly landing if he had to, but without power and at least one engine, the plane... and possibly their lives... would be lost.

He continued to descend fairly quickly as he got closer.

Just as the small community came into view the radio lit up with an excited voice.

"Unknown aircraft please identify!"

This took Mark by surprise, but he said, "This is ERA flight 1690 out of Anchorage. My right engine has cut out and I'm on reserve fuel at this time, requesting immediate landing instructions."

"ERA flight 1690, uh..., we have no record of you on any schedule. You will need to explain yourself upon landing. You are clear for the runway in front of you."

After descending farther Mark slowed his airspeed and started to lower the flaps. The left engine continued to run as he skipped across the less-than adequate gravel landing strip and taxied to the largest hangar near a small radio tower. Before getting out of the aircraft he retrieved some silver bars and gold coins from his pack and put them in a pocket on his tactical vest.

Andy woke up and groggily asked, "Where are we?"

"A small village on the coast. I'm going to get us fueled up and back in the air. Stay here with Schnell."

Andy did as he was instructed, and after looking out the windows on both sides Mark opened the door of the plane.

He was met by an older Alaska State Trooper with thin, wired glasses. Next to him were a couple of men in suits, to which he didn't pay much attention.

Upon exiting the bullet-ridden plane, the trooper became very nervous at the sight of him. Mark had grown a thicker beard, and with the gear and weapons he had about his person, he looked intimidating, to say the least.

"Sir, please put your hands up," insisted the excited cop with his hand on top of his sidearm.

"Mister," began Mark as he slowly walked closer, "I've had it with people trying to tell me what to do and point guns at me as you're about to. I just need some fuel for my aircraft and I'll be on my merry way."

"You're going to answer some questions first," said a tall man in a suit and overcoat.

"Listen," Mark began in a frustrated tone as Schnell started to growl at the men from the open door. "The world has come to an end and it's a free-for-all out there. Most U.S. cities have been destroyed and martial law didn't do any good. If you don't know what's going on, then you need to send some scouts out to get information. I don't have the patience to sit here and talk to you boys. Now, I'm going to reach into my vest pocket and get out some bars of silver to barter with. Don't shoot me, slick," he said to the trooper, "because I will shoot back."

Mark pulled out a few silver bars and a gold coin to seal the deal and motioned for a short man in a suit to walk over. He handed him the currency and asked for a full tank of avgas.

"Yes, sir," said the man, who walked inside to get someone to operate the truck and dispense the fuel.

The trooper walked over and asked, "Who are you?"

"Just a weary traveler, friend."

The two men stood and talked by the fuel truck while it filled the plane's tanks. Mark gave him as much information as he could remember.

"A little over a week ago I was running missions all over Afghanistan and never thought the things

I had prepared for here at home would ever actually happen."

"So the Russians have invaded Alaska and other countries have invaded other parts of the U.S., too?" asked the trooper as he tried to wrap his head around everything Mark was telling him.

"It's been a wild week and many people have lost their lives."

"Anyone you know personally, like family? We've been stuck here without word from the outside since all of our communications went down."

"I lost some close friends," said Mark, trying to leave the conversation. "Looks like I'm about ready to get going."

The fuel truck was pulling away after the operator got done filling the plane's tanks. Mark thanked everyone, got in the aircraft and was soon in the air and on his way east once again.

"What did they talk to you about?" asked Andy after the plane stopped climbing and he had unbuckled and walked to the cockpit.

"They haven't had any contact with the outside world since this all started and wanted to know everything I knew, and more."

"I'm getting hungry. Would you like me to make you something?"

"If you could make me a sandwich, that would be great," replied Mark.

The two of them sat in the cockpit with the plane on autopilot and enjoyed a small meal of ham sandwiches.

"They were military men," Andy piped up suddenly.

"Who?" questioned Mark, knowing what he meant, but wanting him to talk about it more. He knew it would help him start to emotionally deal with the situation.

"The men who came to the lodge."

"What military? Did they have flags or any identifying marks?"

"I'm not sure, but there was one man who looked different than the rest. He had a long black beard and was wearing a strange-looking hat."

"Did he act like he was in charge?"

"No, not really, he just stood back and watched."

Mark had more information than he had before and didn't want to push.

Who was the mystery man with the beard? he thought.

He thanked Andy for the food and checked over the instruments as Andy went to see how Schnell was doing.

They were able to fly to Prince George Airport in British Columbia. This time there was no contact on the radio. Mark knew the town wasn't as remote, and definitely larger than Icy Bay, but why was no one around? He circled the town looking for signs of life and, finally, when they found nothing moving, he lined up with the main landing strip.

As soon as he touched down Mark taxied toward the terminal and shut the engines down. He, Andy and Schnell got out and surveyed the immediate vicinity.

"Still nothing, girl?" he asked her softly.

"Where is everyone?" questioned Andy.

He searched for a fuel truck, but found none. He located a fueling station with underground tanks, but with no power on he couldn't access the vital element.

They walked into the building, looked around a bit, then went out front. There were a few vehicles in the parking lot so he decided to take a blue Toyota 4 Runner with oversize tires and a ten inch lift. If he had to go off road for any reason, he figured this should get the job done.

The doors were locked so he broke out one of the small rear windows to gain entry. Once he got the driver's side door open, he went to work locating the wires under the dash with which he could start the truck.

A few short minutes later the Toyota came to life and its purring beckoned Mark to take it for a ride. He drove around the main building to the plane. They unloaded their supplies from the aircraft. Andy opened the passenger door, Schnell jumped in and they drove off toward town to locate gas. Power was out everywhere, so they would have to find a hand pump or siphon gas out of other vehicles.

The second option is what eventually had to happen. Once he got some extra 5-gallon cans and a small hose from the local hardware store, Mark went to work siphoning fuel out of several vehicles to reach his desired goal. He was light headed and sick to his stomach when done.

Driving would be slower and more dangerous, but for now this was the only option available to them.

They went through the town and gathered as many supplies as they could find that hadn't been looted. Schnell led the way into each building. Dry and non-perishable food was scarce but they found enough to last a short time. It appeared that the town had cleared out in a hurry, and the stores were pretty empty.

Night was falling but Mark decided they should head out anyway.

The road was completely clear for many miles ahead. They followed Highway 16 east toward Alberta. The drive would take them into the Columbia Mountains and a few small towns.

Sometime the next morning, just before entering the small town of Jasper, Schnell perked up and growled, waking Andy. A few seconds later, Mark understood why she was acting like that.

Chapter Thirty-Five

Yukon Territory
Day 9
Mark, Andy and Schnell

The roadblock looked like it consisted of law enforcement, military and civilians. Mark wished he had noticed the line of vehicles ahead of time. He was too close now to turn around without arousing suspicion and would have to take his chances. He pulled the small blanket out from under Schnell to cover his tactical gear from view and removed his Glock from its holster. He put the gun in his lap just in case he needed to use it.

Mark methodically surveyed the scene in front of him to make a mental escape plan as he continued on.

"Andy, you do exactly as I say and don't talk unless you're asked to."

He inched closer and was the fourth vehicle in line when an officer in a dirty uniform approached the driver's side of their truck.

Schnell moved closer to the window as he approached and a low growl started in her throat.

"Easy, girl," Mark murmured. "Just let it happen."

She did as she was told, laying her head down on the seat and didn't even look up when the man approached the door.

"Where you headed, buddy?" he asked with a slight French accent as he poked his head closer to look inside, but Mark didn't roll the window all the way down.

"Just trying to get away from all the violence," replied Mark.

"Do you two have any weapons on you?"

"No, sir, I don't, but I wish I did."

"Oh yea, why's that?"

"To protect myself, my son and my dog, of course," said Mark.

"I see. Why do you have that blanket wrapped around you?"

"The heater stopped working when we were coming out of the mountains," replied Mark as he looked over, making eye contact with the man.

"I need you to get out of the vehicle," he told Mark as he motioned with his hand and more men headed toward them.

"I have a hurt leg and can't really do that right now."

The man pulled a Beretta 92 9-mm pistol with a small silencer on it out of his waistband, pointed it at Mark's head and said, "Get out now, or we make a mess right here with ya."

"I wouldn't do that if I were you."

"And what are you going to do about it, eh?"

"Andy, you should duck."

"Huh?" questioned the man with the gun.

Mark slowly moved his head forward as the silencer was pushed against his left side, then with one fluid motion he moved out of the way of the gun as a round was fired. It was deafeningly loud that close to Mark's ear and the bullet broke the passenger side window. Glass shards flew everywhere as he grabbed the top of the slide, pushing it toward the man. The man pulled the trigger, but nothing happened. Mark flipped the take down lever with his thumb, and to the man's amazement, pulled the slide off the frame, leaving the grip frame in his hand with the ammunition from the magazine staring back at him.

"What the...," he started.

As he backed away from the truck in confusion, Mark shot him through the door with his Glock, to try and muffle the noise, but it wasn't enough. A firefight erupted from both sides of the road with the other men shooting at the truck. Muzzle flashes could be seen and bullets were hitting all over the vehicle. From inside, Mark could hear bullets breaking glass and punching holes in the truck. He pushed the accelerator, ramming the small Toyota Camry in front of him, to move it out of the way.

He backed up as more bullets penetrated the windshield, making it harder to see, and maneuvered to the side of the road past the road block. A man stepped in front of the truck about thirty meters away and opened fire with an AK-47 on full auto. Bullets hit with a loud *thump-thump-thump-thump* as Mark pushed the truck as fast as it would go and hit the man, sending him over the hood and into the windshield. He slammed the brakes and moved the broken glass out of his view after the man rolled off the hood. Mark hit the gas again, running him over. He heard his muffled scream, then silence as the rear tires went over him like they were driving over a small log. Mark then sped off down the road.

Just a few short kilometers later, steam was rolling from under the hood. The engine had overheated and the vehicle lurched to a stop. He, Andy and Schnell got out and gathered as many supplies as they could carry. Mark walked a short distance, stopped and looked back at the bullet-ridden truck with no windshield and two flat tires, while saying to Schnell, "How did we get out of that one, girl?"

They walked down the road for many kilometers before coming to a well-maintained gravel road to the right. He took out his binoculars and could see a ranch in the distance beyond a cluster of trees. The chance had to be taken to obtain shelter so they could rest.

The long road leading up to the main house had perfect line of sight for a sniper if one was there. He knew they were asking for it, but there was no other choice.

As they approached the house, a man came out with a shotgun pointed at them.

"That's far enough," said the older man wearing dirty coveralls. His long graying beard was blowing in the slight afternoon breeze.

Being tired from traveling so far without much sleep, Mark knew that Schnell could easily overpower the old man with a simple command, and besides, what choice did he have at this point? He saw no need to end the man's journey just for a few hours of rest and a little food.

Mark did as he was told and dropped his gear and weapons. "We wish you no harm, sir," he said as he backed away from his belongings, pulling Andy back, too. "I just need a place for me, my son and my dog to rest for a while."

"We don't want any trouble, son," said the man.

"We don't want any either, sir."

"Where'd you all come from?"

"Actually, we came from Alaska."

"Really?" asked the man as he got even closer. "And why are you here?"

"The plane I was flying ran out of fuel and I had to ditch it at Prince George Airport."

The man picked up Mark's rifle and handguns, then motioned for them to follow. "Grab your belongings and follow me," he said. "We can give you a place to rest for the night, but you need to be on your way by morning. Maggie will be starting lunch soon if you're hungry."

"We are, sir, thank you."

"Stop calling me 'sir,' boy. The name's Leonard, Leonard Pickens, and this is my land. It's been in the family for five generations. I will hold on to your guns until you're ready to leave. That is how I want things."

"I understand," said Mark.

The four of them walked inside and introductions were made. Leonard's wife was cooking something in the oven that smelled good as they entered.

"This is Maggie," said Leonard. "And this dirty gentleman is...What was your name again, son?"

"Mark Mitchell, and this is my son, Andy, and my loyal companion, Schnell. It's very nice to meet the both of you."

Maggie was a thin, frail older woman who wore thick glasses and had a limp on her right side. Her shorter, graying hair was pulled back in a small ponytail.

"You are a beautiful German shepherd," she said to Schnell as she called her over and began to pet her.

Leonard showed Mark and Andy to the bedroom in which they would sleep and Schnell followed.

Mark thanked him and proceeded to put his gear down.

"You can wash up down the hall."

"Thank you for your hospitality."

The man stared at Andy briefly, then walked away without saying a word. Mark felt comfortable here and decided to take a shower and shave while he had the chance.

"I'm going to go downstairs," informed Andy.

Mark knew that the boy was still trying to process everything that had happened and let him do his thing.

Schnell stood guard just inside the door as he turned the water on and got undressed.

He looked in the mirror as the shower heated up. His beard was getting long and his hair was growing back, at least where he wasn't going bald. He trimmed it all the best he could.

The hot water and smell of the soap were like heaven to him. It had only been about a week since everything had started, but it felt like much longer. Dirty water and soap bubbles were filling the bottom of the shower at first, and then slowly turned clear.

Once he felt clean Mark turned the water off and grabbed a towel. He noticed that his clothes were gone and a pair of folded coveralls was in their place. Schnell was gone too. He didn't feel very comfortable wearing them but had nothing else to put on. He went to the room and noticed his other clothes were missing, as well. Everything he had in his pockets was laid out perfectly on the bed.

He went downstairs, where he found the old couple sitting at the table with Schnell sitting by Maggie.

"He doesn't look too bad at all in those clothes," commented Maggie. "I put your dirty clothes in the wash. I hope you don't mind."

"No, ma'am," said Mark, looking around. "Thank you, and I see you made a new friend."

"She is wonderful," said Maggie with a smile.

"The boy is out back," said Leonard. "Do you mind me asking what's wrong with him?"

"He has seen too much violence recently. His parents were killed by the Russians and he is trying to deal with all of it."

The couple understood, or tried to. Mark was able to get Andy back inside and they all enjoyed a nice afternoon meal. Maggie had made a cottage pie with fresh vegetables from her garden. Mark told them his story as they ate and he listened to what they knew.

While waiting for his clothes to be done he relaxed on the porch swing with Schnell by his side. He reflected about the past few weeks, starting back in Afghanistan through all the events that led up to what brought him to where he was now.

"You OK son?" Leonard asked as he walked out on the porch to smoke his pipe.

"As good as can be expected," replied Mark.

"Life throws in little twists for us so we don't get too bored. At least that's how I look at it."

"Well, I suppose I haven't been very bored lately, then," he said with a slight grin.

"There you go," said Maggie as she walked out the door with a pipe in her hand, also. "You need to smile sometimes, or your face will get stuck with that mean look on it."

They all chuckled a little and talked for a while longer before Mark decided to go up and inventory his gear. Andy stayed outside and played fetch with Schnell.

"I'll let you know when supper is ready, son," said Maggie before he walked inside.

Much to his surprise, his M4 and his two pistols were laid out on the bed next to his clean clothes, which he changed back into.

They must feel comfortable with us in order to give the weapons back, he thought. He decided to just leave it as it was and not say anything.

After a nice evening with his new acquaintances Mark retired to his room with the promise of a restful night's sleep.

Andy had been in the room for some time already. He was fast asleep under the blankets, so Mark just lay down on top of his side, pulled his Barrett cap over his eyes and eventually fell asleep.

He was awakened in the early morning hours by doors slamming and yelling from downstairs.

"What now?" he whispered to Schnell as he quickly got dressed and looked at his watch. It said it was just after 0400.

"Stay here, Andy, but get dressed and be ready to move if need be."

He put his body armor and tactical gear on and went downstairs very quietly.

He counted five men with guns as he got to the bottom of the stairs. The Pickens couple was sitting on the couch in front of them. They held each other tightly. Maggie had buried her head in Leonard's shirt out of obvious fear. Mark could see that they were dragged out of bed. They both had flannel night gowns on. They were scared out of their minds.

Mark felt confident that he could take the men out before they could get a shot off. He yelled a command for Schnell, "Csibesz," and she bolted to "get him" as instructed.

This also got the men's attention, as Mark turned on his weapon light and blinded them with the strobe feature so he could shoot. Schnell attacked one of the men and Mark shot the others. He moved and fired at the same time so they couldn't get a fix on him.

Loud, *thwack-thwack-thwacks* were heard, and then muzzle flashes and yelling from the men could be seen and heard from different areas of the poorly lit room as Mark engaged, but his bright weapon light gave him the advantage that he needed, until all threats were eliminated.

He finished off the man that his canine companion had subdued, with a single shot to the head from his Glock. The man was begging for his life before Mark ended it.

He then looked over at the old couple. They had both somehow been shot in the firefight. They sat on the couch bleeding out and trying to say something. Mark heard a faint, "Thank you," from Maggie before her last breath left her. Mark closed their eyes and just as he and Schnell went to look through the rest of the house to make sure no one else was there, they heard a creaking noise from the stairs. Andy was standing there staring at the scene in the living room.

"I'm sorry, son, I tried to help them."

Andy just walked back upstairs and slowly closed the bedroom door.

As soon as it was light enough outside, Mark took the couple out to bury them and disposed of the others behind the barn.

He and Schnell just stood over the hole he had dug with Leonard's tractor. Mark had a solemn look on his face and then shook his head before getting back on the piece of equipment and pushing the dirt in to fill the void.

Once the task was completed he went inside and found the keys to the Chevy Suburban on the side of the house. Luckily, the fuel tank read almost full. He loaded all his belongings and what food was in the house into the vehicle, Schnell jumped in the passenger seat and moved over when Andy got in. They left the ranch behind them for what Mark hoped was a better place. The idea at this point was to find the *Safe Zone* promised on the radio and hopefully outlast what was going on in the world.

After a few hours he passed the turn off for Highway 11 east. A couple kilometers later he noticed a large, black truck in the rear-view mirror. The vehicle continued to get closer, even as Mark accelerated. He was going 140 kilometers an hour when the large truck caught up with him and rammed the back of the Suburban. Then the truck came around his right side, and what he saw behind them made him wonder if they were going to be able to escape this one.

Chapter Thirty-Six

Somewhere in British Columbia
Day 10
Mark, Andy and Schnell

Another jacked-up truck, a red one, had been following the black one, and only came into view when the first one moved to the side. Both trucks had massive bumpers welded on the front, specifically designed for ramming. They had racks built on top of them and metal plates with slots covering the windows. Mark imagined that they had been up-armored as well.

With lawlessness running rampant, it was inevitable that people would be banding together and taking what they wanted.

"It's about to get interesting, girl!"

Schnell barked in agreement.

"Hang on, Andy!"

The black truck moved toward Mark and tried pushing him to the shoulder, while the red one slammed into the rear end repeatedly. No matter how much more he accelerated there was no way he could match the power of the diesel engines that were pushing the trucks.

Mark pointed his M4 out the window, letting a full auto burst fly at the black truck's front end. It immediately retreated to the rear, and then slid off the road, while the red one hit him again from behind.

He knew they would eventually run him off the road or damage his vehicle so badly that he would have no choice but to pull over, so he did just that. A few hundred meters up the highway was a gravel turn off. Mark slowed down just enough so he wouldn't roll, and as he hit the gravel he turned the wheel and slid sideways to a complete stop. The red truck slammed into the driver's door just as Mark exited the passenger side, pushing Andy out, with Schnell on his heels. The truck was pushed several meters and came to a stop just before Mark's face.

"Marad," Mark said to Schnell, commanding her to "stay" so she didn't get shot.

He moved to engage, staying low around the rear of the truck for cover, and as soon as the doors started to open he fired quickly, with the occupants of the truck firing back. Smoke from all the spent powder was beginning to make it hard to see, as his M4 ran dry quickly. He made a tactical magazine change with the empty one bouncing off the gravel, and then continued to engage until nothing was moving. His M4 was out, the bolt was open and the muzzle was smoking from so many rounds having been fired so quickly, so Mark drew his Glock which was faster than reloading his rifle at that point.

The fight was over very fast, as all four occupants had exited the red truck. They lay in pools of blood outside the vehicle. There were two men, a woman and a teenage boy. They had all been threats that were shooting at him, so he did what he needed to do and felt no guilt or remorse. Schnell was running about the bodies sniffing.

He holstered his sidearm, then reloaded a fresh mag once more in his rifle, closing the bolt and chambering a round. Mark moved to check if there was anyone else inside. Seeing that the vehicle was empty he started throwing his gear into the cab. A noise from down the highway got his attention as he and Andy loaded the last of their stuff into the red truck. The black one was re-engaging them, so he closed all doors, got in after Schnell and Andy did, and headed down the road.

He pushed the accelerator to the floor, but the black truck continued to gain on him. They were so close that people could be seen in the mirrors, crawling out the windows of the black truck, and soon started shooting at them. Mark figured they were trying to hit the rear tires and force him to stop, so he slammed on the brakes, making the black truck ram his back bumper. The jolt sent Schnell into the back seat, while one of the occupants of the other truck fell off and could be seen skidding across the asphalt, then rolling off the road completely

Mark accelerated again, and the black truck came at him once more. The people were relentless in the pursuit, but it was a good thing that he was well versed in combat driving.

The road began to narrow as the fight continued, then started to turn into curve after curve and climbed uphill.

"This might be our chance, girl!" yelled Mark enthusiastically.

The black truck stayed back and the people just kept shooting, so he slowed down to draw them in.

He continued to slow down, then slammed on the brakes. He put the transmission in reverse and pushed the black truck backward. He cut the wheel hard and pushed them through the guard rail. The truck slid down the gravel embankment and started rolling. It hit the bottom of the ravine below, upside down, and the wheels kept turning because the engine was still on. Mark got out and fired at the fuel tank until it caught fire. A few seconds later it blew up. He didn't see anyone get out of the wreckage as it burned, and eventually got back in his new vehicle and drove on down the road.

"What is wrong with people?" he asked his companion. "They were crazy before the world ended and now they're just insane."

He stared at Schnell for a moment, waiting for a response that he knew he wouldn't get, but waited anyway.

Andy just sat there in his usual silent state. Mark knew he would eventually need to address everything that had happened so the boy could move on.

They resumed travel down the lonely stretch of highway for many more kilometers without incident. A sign on the side of the road said "Lake Louise 2- kilometers." Mark was sure that he hadn't seen any other signs previously, but he had been a little pre-occupied.

The closer they got to the next town, the more houses could be seen along the highway. As they drove around another bend in the road Mark got a bewildered look on his face and tapped the brakes to slow down.

"Are we ever going to catch a break?" he asked Schnell.

Chapter Thirty-Seven

British Columbia
Mark, Andy and Schnell

About 500 meters in front of them was another road block. There were too many people manning this one to fight it out. A couple of school buses and other vehicles were stacked together to block the highway and the sides all the way to the tree line, so ramming it was not an option.

Mark had slowed down considerably, but had not come to a stop yet, and figured they were already in the ambush zone, so he continued on. Much to his surprise one of the buses just backed out of the way to let the large red truck pass. Without any hesitation, Mark poured on the speed and went right on through.

"Hell yes!" he yelled. "They must have just thought that we were their friends coming back from a day on the road."

Schnell's ears perked up, and she cocked her head sideways when Mark acted so excited.

Reducing speed they drove slowly into the small town where there were people milling about like nothing had happened to the rest of the world. He knew he shouldn't stop since he wasn't the owner of the truck, but they needed fuel and could use some rest, too.

Some of the buildings along what appeared to be the main street were boarded up and as they past the last one they saw less people. There were a few houses just passed the main cluster, so he decided to pull into one of the driveways and seek refuge.

Just after turning in and driving up to the main house of the little farm, a few men walked out the front door with AK-47s. Mark stopped the truck and put it in park when he saw a flag flying on a pole near the house. It looked like the same insignia as the tattoos he had seen and the lapel pin Travis had described.

"What the hell is going on?" he muttered softly.

He shut the engine off and sat there watching them. Two of the men started walking toward him and one man spoke in a Middle-Eastern tongue that Mark immediately recognized. "Syed, why are you just sitting there? Come on out and tell us how the day went."

This confirmed what Mark was thinking about the residents here, and then some. Some might be good people just trying to survive, but the rest were hunting people down on the roads and slaughtering them to take what they had. And that, Mark wasn't going to stand for. The insignia on the flag was still a conundrum. Was this a real thing, or organization?

They obviously couldn't see inside the cab with the tinted windows and welded steel shutters.

"I've got this one, girl," said Mark as he opened the driver's side door, Glock in hand, and shot the first two men point blank in their faces *pop, pop*. As blood sprayed from the large wounds in the soft flesh they fell motionless to the ground, dropping their rifles. The other one that had lingered back by the porch just stared in disbelief as Mark slid out of the driver's seat and fired two fast shots at him, hitting him center mass. The young man slumped down by the stairs and silently passed. Schnell jumped out and started doing a recon of the area as Mark moved inside with Andy right behind him.

Once satisfied that there was no one else around, he sat at the kitchen table and started wolfing down the food that the three men had been eating for lunch. It was something he recognized and had eaten before. Qabili Palau, a dish from Afghanistan that consisted of chicken topped with fried raisins, slivered carrots and pistachios.

"You're just going to eat their food after killing them? What is that, anyway?" Andy asked.

"You want some?" Mark asked Andy, barely making sense because of his full mouth. "It's actually pretty good."

"It looks disgusting!"

Mark just laughed. Feeling his hunger pangs subsiding, the tired professional soldier knew that it was only a matter of time until he was forced into a position that he might not make it out of. He put the plate on the floor and Schnell finished it off. Mark poured some water in a bowl from the kitchen faucet, which she slurped down as if it was going to run away from her.

"Let's go find some fuel and get out of here," he said to Andy and his companion. She barked, showing her approval, and they all walked outside.

A fuel tank was located on the side of one of the outbuildings, so Mark went back to get the truck in order to fill up.

It didn't take long to top off the large auxiliary tank in the bed and the factory one underneath. The pump poured the off-road diesel into the reservoirs at a fast rate.

Just as Mark was screwing the cap down on the tank in the bed, Schnell started growling, and then he heard the vehicles approaching.

"Inside, now!" he ordered.

They all jumped in the cab and Mark started it up as Andy sat in the back seat looking scared. Two smaller trucks came into view and about half a dozen men got out. They were looking at the bodies by the house when the large red truck started moving in their direction. The men started shooting with AK-47's set on full auto, as Mark just accelerated more while firing his M4 out of a hole in the window. He hit both trucks, one after the other, in hopes of putting them out of commission. Suddenly, he felt a sensation like a bee sting in his left shoulder. With his adrenalin pumping, he ignored it and kept going. Once he entered the highway again, more vehicles were starting to pursue him as he made his escape out of the area. Just down the road was another road block, but this one was smaller, with less people. He changed magazines in his rifle and once they got closer he started shooting out of a hole in the windshield. He easily smashed through the line of vehicles blocking the road, as a hail of bullets smacked against the truck, most of them ricocheting off the steel plates covering the windows.

A few minutes later, with no one else in pursuit, Mark grabbed his arm that had begun to hurt even more. He felt the wetness, then looked at the crimson color on his hand.

"That's just great," he said as he pulled over to the side of the road. He reached into his bag and, after a little searching, found a packet of Quick-Clot. He poured the whole package onto the wound through the tear in his sleeve and winced in pain as the bleeding was being stopped by the hemostatic agent.

"How're you doing back there, Andy?" he asked.

Mark turned around and saw that Andy had been shot, too, and lost consciousness

Mark moved quickly into the back seat to assess Andy's wound. He had taken a round in his right upper chest, but closer to his shoulder than lungs.

After checking it out, Mark came to the realization that the bullet must have lost too much velocity after punching through the window before entering him. He would need to remove the slug soon or Andy would die from the infection.

After applying a pack of Quick-Clot to the wound, he took the medical kit out of his pack and went to work on retrieving the bullet. Mark cut an incision large enough to get the forceps in and began searching for the bullet. He knew it would hurt like hell if Andy woke up, but he was finally able to find it before he did. It had lodged itself about an inch in and had stopped on his scapula. Without an x-ray there was no way to tell if it had fractured the bone. Mark irrigated the wound with saline and put a sterile bandage on it.

Mark secured Andy in a seatbelt, put everything away and started in the direction of the *Safe Zone*. After getting back on the road, he drove for several more hours trying to put even more distance between them and the last town. The drive was un-eventful, as he saw no other vehicles or signs of life.

The fuel gauge was showing signs that it might be faulty as he got closer to the small town of Banff. It was registering almost empty, and it shouldn't be. He swapped over to the reservoir tank in the bed with the flip of a switch and the gauge ran back up to full. It was soon falling back down, so he pulled over, only to realize that a bullet must have penetrated the main tank. There was a trail of fuel as far down the road as he could see. Getting back in he didn't waste any time driving as far as he was able to.

Smoke could be seen on the horizon as they came out of the mountains. Mark could see that this was an isolated town surrounded by tall peaks, and was surprised at what he saw.

From what he could tell as he rolled in on fumes, the town of Banff was deserted and much of the area was destroyed by fire. Mark found a filling station and pulled in. Much of this structure was still intact, which was good.

Schnell jumped out once they stopped and, after relieving herself, checked the area.

Mark walked through the maintenance section of the gas station until he found a hand pump and a long section of hose, along with a few rags and some Bondo that he hoped would work as a patch. He hooked the hose onto the pump with a clamp and walked out to the truck. The tank had stopped leaking and was now empty, so he wiped the spot clean and mixed the materials together to make a patch. He couldn't see an exit, so it must have been a fragment from a ricochet that had just punched a hole in the tank.

Once the patch was dry, he pumped the last of the fuel he could get out of the station's above-ground tanks into the truck, then Mark did an inventory of ammo. He knew that after the last battle with the road gangs that he was pretty low, but didn't realize that his M4 was completely dry and the bolt was open. He looked through all of the magazine pouches on his vest and found them all to be empty. He emptied out his dump pouch and found those mags were all empty too. All pistol mags were found to be empty, as well, so he checked his Glock. A round in the chamber and a half-full mag left in the gun was it. Not enough to do much with, but he would do the best he could if he encountered any more resistance on the road.

Andy was still out cold and Mark was tired, but needed to push on. He and Schnell got in the bullet-ridden truck and continued on their journey.

The drive from British Columbia across to Alberta was long and hard. Andy was in and out of consciousness the whole time. They had stopped a couple of times down small side roads with dead ends so Mark could rest, but he didn't really sleep. Being wounded and tired had taken its toll on Mark. The bleeding had stopped, but without food and water for the last two days he was very weak. He had given Andy the last of their water because his wound was worse and he needed it.

The plan was getting over the mountains and hoping to find refuge in Calgary, where he thought the radio transmission might have originated from. But to see the devastation laid out in front of him going through Banff and then Canmore was more than he could handle. Mark finally lost it, pulled over and got out. He fell to his knees and started screaming. Tears were running down his bruised and dirty cheeks. His heart sank to its lowest level. Schnell came over to console him licking the tears from his face, as she felt his pain. He had thought of using the last round in his sidearm on himself, but as the bright red sun came up, shining through the trees, and another day dawned he figured he would see what it brought. The bright colors of morning danced above the surrounding mountains, and the chirping of a few small birds brought on the sensation of life continuing. They had come this far and had to make their way to Calgary and hope that something remained.

Chapter Thirty-Eight

Alberta Territory, Canada, 'The Safe Zone'
Day 11
Mark, Andy and Schnell

Mark saw more signs of civilization the closer they got to Calgary on the Trans-Canada Highway, with more traffic seen traveling in both directions. The farms and ranches on the prairie were being worked, as well. Large sprinklers were spewing water far distances and tractors tilled the soil. This all made sense for planting crops this time of year, but he still felt uneasy about it because until now, nothing had been normal.

The feathery cirrus clouds hanging high above the valley floor were giving way to more blue sky, and bright rays of light shown down on the prairie. The temperature continued to rise and heat waves were seen dancing in the distance.

"Life seems somewhat normal here, except for the guard towers near the fields," Mark said to Schnell in a concerned tone as they passed another one.

She barked in agreement, which woke up Andy.

"Mark," he spoke in a low, rough voice. "What's going on?"

"You were shot a couple days ago and we've been on the road ever since."

"Where are we going?"

"The *Safe Zone* is still the plan. How're you feeling?"

"I'm in a lot of pain."

"I know you are. As soon as we get into the city, we're going straight to a hospital."

The fuel gauge was close to empty when the Petro Canada gas station came into view. A few vehicles were at the pumps and more were parked near the building. Mark also saw a dozen or so tractor trailers parked out back as they pulled up to the pumps.

"We're going to stop and fuel up. If they have any food I'll get you some. You and Schnell stay here."

The gas station was just a few kilometers outside the city center of Calgary to the east. The city had a population of over 1 million people before the attack on the United States. Most things seemed normal here, too, except the guard tower. Mark decided to take off his tactical gear and leave it in the truck so not to draw any unwanted attention, but tucked his Beretta under his shirt.

Andy sat up and looked out the window as Mark disappeared into the building. Most of the people outside looked dirty and tired, but some were very well dressed.

Mark soon returned, started the pump next to the truck and began to fill up. Many of the people were staring at him as he did so. After topping off all tanks he got back in and threw Andy a candy bar, and a bottle of water.

"What's going on out there?"

"I know what you mean. There were many more of them inside, too. The counter man gave me directions to the *Safe Zone*. It shouldn't take long to get there. I was told they have a hospital set up inside."

Mark started the truck and drove toward the city to find help for Andy, even though his neck hairs were standing at attention because of what he saw around them. He slowed down once he noticed signs pointing the way to their destination just a few short kilometers away.

No road blocks were found on the highway, but as they got closer to the city, walls, barbed-wire fences and more guard towers could be seen skirting a massive compound surrounding the old complex from the 1988 winter Olympics where the *Safe Zone* had been set up. The center housed the Canada Olympic Parks main complex. The mostly destroyed Calgary skyline stood in the background, with only a couple of the skyscrapers still visible, and most just barely. The scene was surreal at best. Light gray smoke rose from parts of the city.

"So far it looks like there weren't many places to hide from the attacks," Mark said to Andy, as he slowed down even more.

Traffic was slightly thicker here as they entered the road leading to the complex. There were no more signs. Men carrying weapons, wearing matching blue BDU's, and black berets took their place. Mark started having more reservations about the "*Safe Zone*." The men in uniforms directed people to park in certain areas after talking with them at the entrance.

Mark rolled down his window as he came to a rough-looking man with a goatee. He had his hand raised and was giving signals.

"You guys are a welcome sight."

"Sir, do you have any identification on you?"

"I sure don't, but I can tell you anything you want to know."

"Please take a left up there by those gentlemen."

Mark could see where he was pointing and did as asked. After being told where to park, a few men approached the truck.

"Sir, please shut the engine off," requested a tall, thin man in a crisp blue uniform, with sergeant stripes on his sleeves. He approached the vehicle holding his rifle out in front of him like the others, a tan, FNH SCAR 16 chambered in 5.56x45 mm, which Mark recognized.

Mark did as instructed and then waited patiently for the next command he knew was coming.

They all approached the driver's door and through his remaining mirrors, he could see others boxing him in on all sides.

"Where did you come from?" questioned a shorter man who, after taking off his Ray-Ban sunglasses, had a knife scar that ran across his face, from his chin up to the bottom of his left eye.

"We just drove down from Alaska where things were real bad."

"Is there anyone else in the vehicle?"

"My son is in the back seat, he has a gunshot wound that needs attention, and my dog here," replied Mark as Schnell poked her head out the window, tongue flopping in the warm morning air.

"Do you have any weapons on you?"

"Not on me, but I do here in the truck."

"Please exit the vehicle slowly and ask your son to do the same. Restrain your dog if you're able. If it attacks we will have no choice but to put it down."

"That won't be necessary."

They did as they were asked while the other men took up positions for a possible engagement. They seemed to be ready for anything. Mark recognized many things the guys were doing right, and few they did wrong.

Obviously they were well trained, but who trained them? Military? Law enforcement? The ones that spoke have perfect Western American accents, but they seem Eastern European with some of their actions and looks, Mark thought.

Once they were all out, they were searched for weapons while the truck was gone through.

"Sergeant, please take these men to gate Alpha Two," said Scarface.

"Roger that, sir," said the young man, who looked very eager to please.

"Please leave everything and come with me, gentlemen."

The young soldier or whatever he was, escorted them to a line of people that was slowly entering a gate on the southeast side of the compound.

Mark knew that his gear, valuables and weapons might be lost for good, but Andy needed antibiotics or he would die a horrible death.

"So what can you tell us about what's happened here and in America?" Mark asked, trying to get anything from him.

"Please just keep walking, sir."

These guys are hiding something, thought Mark. *The guard towers near the fields, the one at the fueling station, the use of obvious mercs... If Andy didn't need help, we wouldn't be here. Something is undoubtedly wrong with this whole situation,* he concluded.

The lines and the whole picture in front of them, from the walls and barbed wire to the guard towers, catwalks and the dogs, seemed more like they were entering a German concentration camp. Mark's mind wandered to thoughts of pictures of Auschwitz from World War II.

"Andy, hang on to these for me," said Mark as he took off his dog tags and discreetly passed them to the boy.

"Why do you want me to hang on to...?"

Mark cut him off by nonchalantly pointing out guards on the catwalk above. They passed it a couple minutes later and he began again.

"I just have a feeling here and want to see if I'm right. For now, just tell them that they were your father's and since he was killed in Iraq, you keep them to remember him."

Andy nodded and kept walking.

"Also, you're my stepson, and our last name is Ford. My first name is Stanley."

"Got it," smiled Andy.

The lines congested, the closer they got to the front. Something was happening before they let anyone through the gates. Most of the people that were entering the *Safe Zone* were dirty and wore tattered clothing. Others looked just like a normal person would have before the attacks, wearing clean clothes, like suits and dresses. None of them had bags or suitcases, however. The guards or soldiers, or whatever they were, didn't allow anyone to bring items inside the compound.

"I'm not feeling well," said Andy.

"Just a little farther and we'll be inside and go straight to the medics that I'm sure they have on the other side."

Mark was on edge and his senses were working overtime, processing everything going on around them.

They soon learned as they got near the front of the line that it was a body scanner that was slowing everyone down. Mark knew that Andy wouldn't be able to raise his arms and would be pulled aside.

"Open your shirt and let them see the dry blood."

Andy did as he was told.

On the last catwalk above the gates, something caught Mark's eye. He looked hard to his left through the bright lights shining down on them, and couldn't believe what he saw.

There's no way in hell that he could be here, Mark thought.

Mark searched his memory for the photo of the animal he thought he had just seen.

My god!! If that's Umar Abdul, we're all in trouble, but why the hell is he here in Calgary?

Mark quickly looked for the nearest exit, as he went into survival mode, but realized that the outcome would end badly for too many innocent people.

Easily disarming one of the guards is an option, but how far would that get me? And what about Andy? No, this will just have to play out.

Chapter Thirty-Nine

Calgary, Canada Olympic Park
Mark, Andy and Schnell

As soon as Andy got to the front of the line he showed the guards his gunshot wound. After carefully going through the body scanner, two medics put him on a gurney and took him away.

"That's my son!" said Mark, acting frantic.

"Sir, please let the handler take your dog and step into the body scanner," said a young, very muscular guard, wearing lieutenant bars on the collar of his blouse, and sporting a Patek Philippe watch on his right wrist.

Mark looked to his left as another man in a blue uniform was reaching for Schnell with a muzzle. She growled, which prompted Mark to kneel down and whisper into her ear. Once he got closer she walked over to the handler and let him put the muzzle on.

Mark was noticing small things, like the expensive watches and sun glasses worn by some of the men, which would go unnoticed by most untrained individuals.

The body scanner spun around after he stepped into it and once it was done, Mark was asked to follow some other men to processing, while Schnell was taken elsewhere. The guards on the inside had extendable batons holstered on their sides, for weapons instead of firearms.

None of this sat well with Mark, but what could he do now? He had to get help for Andy.

They passed several rooms as they walked down hall after white hall, until finally coming to an arena that would have been used for hockey. The Plexi-glass that lined the center of the arena was a dead giveaway. There were hundreds of people in different lines. Some were filling out paperwork, some were getting shots. A few people sat up above in the thousands of folding red seats that looked down on the scene.

"Where are you taking me?" questioned Mark.

"Processing," said a young man with no insignia on his blouse, indicating to Mark that he was more than likely a private or of some other low rank, not knowing how their chain of command was set up.

The flag pole in the arena caught Mark's eye instantly. "What's that flag mean? I've seen that insignia before."

"That's the flag of the new world, son," declared a familiar voice.

Mark turned to see a Marine major whom he had served with on a few occasions in different theatres. Luckily with all the dirt and facial hair he now sported, the man didn't recognize him.

"What new world?" asked Mark curiously, but not wanting to draw too much attention.

"That insignia on the flag represents hundreds of years of tradition, and is the face of the future. You will learn all about it in the days and weeks to come."

The major walked away with an entourage in tow.

What the hell is going on? Mark wondered again..

He was escorted to a long line, where he waited his turn while constantly surveying the area. This one ended up being for fingerprinting. "This ought to be good," said Mark softly.

"Sir, please put your thumb in the small square," instructed a slightly older, overweight woman, pointing at the pad, as he approached the table.

She twirled her straight brown hair with her fingers as he placed his thumb on the scanner and a camera took his picture simultaneously.

"Nil!" she shouted, and a man instantly started walking toward her from behind the tables. He pushed his glasses back onto the bridge of his nose as he leaned down to look at the monitor, his tie dangling in front of him.

"What do you have?"

"Nothing came up with his thumb scan."

"Try facial recognition."

A few minutes went by and she said, "Still nothing.

"Sir, please follow me," said the man while motioning to someone behind Mark.

A couple guards closed in and followed them from a distance. They left the area and entered a hallway with multiple rooms off of it. The man swiped a keycard in a slot outside of one of them, that he kept on a retractable lanyard and the door unlocked.

He was put in a white room with a small square table in the center and a hard plastic chair to sit on. There were no windows and a single camera in the top right corner, probably with a panoramic view. Mark understood what was going on. He was in a sweat-box. He would be left there for hours while being monitored. He would be expected to do certain things if he was well trained and used to something like this. His thumbprint and facial scans came back with nothing, which meant that he was either a ghost, or just never fingerprinted, which was highly unlikely, in this day and age.

After about ten minutes he started to fidget with the chair and slowly progressed his façade. He banged on the door, yelled for help, he even hit the door with the chair.

Soon after he calmed down, a very petite but voluptuous redhead walked in with a bottle of water. Her long hair shown like crimson velvet as she grabbed it and pulled it all to one side, exposing her slender neck and pulsing jugular, but Mark was too tired to care.

"Mr....," she started to say, pausing, wanting Mark to finish it.

"Ford, Stanley Ford." He knew she wouldn't offer a name unless he asked for it, but if he didn't, she would think he was just scared.

The name he gave her was that of an old Ford dealership in a couple of parts of Alaska, but since his records were sealed, they didn't know he was lying.

"That's an interesting name sir."

"It's a family name. Generation after generation, we have worked the same homestead ranch in Alaska that I come from."

"That's good. So you're here from Alaska?"

"I sure am."

"And what brought you here?"

"We heard a radio broadcast and headed this way just as soon as we could."

"We?"

"Yes, my son and our German shepherd."

"Yes, the boy you came in with is in the med bay and your dog has been kenneled for now. Both are being taken good care of and as long as you cooperate, they will stay that way."

"What do you want from me?"

"Tell us who you are and what your background consists of."

"I already told you, my name is Stanley Ford and I worked on a ranch. I've never been arrested and never fingerprinted. What else can I tell you?"

There was a knock at the door and a tall, thin man in a three-piece suit walked in, and whispered to the woman while handing her something and touching the radio receiver in his left ear, before leaving quickly.

She closed the door behind the man and walked over to the table, dropping dog tags on it.

"Would these be yours, Mark?"

"I already told you, my name is Stanley Ford. Those belong to Andy's father's who died in Iraq," he replied, without wavering in the slightest.

"Mark Mitchell was alive ten days ago and serving in Afghanistan."

"There must be some kind of mistake. Because as far as I know, that man is dead," Mark assured her, pointing at the tags.

The door to the room opened again, and this time a few men in uniform were waiting. The woman just got up and left after grabbing the dog tags.

"Let's go," said one of the men, an older fellow with short graying hair, but still tough- looking.

"Where *are* we going now?"

"The colonel wants to see you. He finds this whole situation *very* interesting."

Mark got up and followed the men through another maze of hallways. They came to an elevator and after one of the men swiped a keycard at the panel opening the doors, they all got on. Mark was positioned in front with the mercs in the back. The standard annoying music was playing from the speakers and nobody was talking.

They stopped on the sixth floor and the doors opened. More guards were standing there waiting.

"Sir, please exit the elevator and follow the gentleman in front of you," was what he heard from behind him.

Mark walked out into a large room with hallways leading in several directions. He followed the man he was asked to, who led him to an office. The walls along the way had pictures of the Olympians from the different games and the medals that they won for Canada. Large windows showed all that was going on down below as more people looking for help converged on the compound and went through processing.

The man in front, a smaller, muscular-looking guy with short brown hair, opened the door without a keycard and asked Mark to sit in a chair to wait.

The use of key cards and where they were used was vital information. *If I can just get my hands on one of those,* Mark thought.

A few minutes later, a side door to the office opened and in walked a large man with full-bird, colonel-rank insignias on his black BDU collars. He had a buzz cut, a thin black mustache, and what looked like a Cuban cigar hanging out of the right side of his mouth. He set a folder down that said "classified" on the outside jacket.

Mark caught himself quickly. He almost stood up at attention upon seeing the man with such a high rank.

Old habits die hard, he thought.

"Son," started the colonel, before sitting down. "I'm told that you didn't come up in any data base when your thumb print was run, or on facial recognition for that matter. This is very interesting to me, because your back-story...*well*, it just don't add up. Feel free to chime in anytime."

A few smart-ass remarks came to mind, but Mark decided to play it cool instead. "I really don't know what to tell you besides what I already have."

Mark recognized the man as a Marine that went missing in action from a forward operating base a few years ago somewhere in the Hindu Kush mountains of Afghanistan. He didn't know all the details, but from what he remembered the FOB came under heavy insurgent attack in the early morning hours and many Marines paid the ultimate sacrifice. The Colonel was one of five Marines MIA from that incursion. Three SEAL teams were flown in to search for the men, mainly due to the high rank of the colonel. After almost a week of searching and one whole SEAL team being shot down in their helo, the search was called off and none of the Marines were found, dead or alive.

Mark could see the patience on the man's face wearing thin.

"Son, we can do this the easy way or the hard way. I think you know what I mean too."

"I'm just a simple man that has come here for help."

"I can see we're going to do this the hard way," said the colonel as he picked up the phone on his desk.

"All right…" began Mark as he was interrupted.

Chapter Forty

Calgary, Canada Olympic Park
Mark Mitchell, contractor

"Mark," said the colonel opening up the folder in front of him "I know this is you. Mark Edward Mitchell, born Dec. 2, 1975. You spent you're last eight years on active duty with 1st Force Recon and have been working for the DOD since you left the Corps. You are airborne and dive qualified, you are proficient in covert ops, intelligence operations and unconventional warfare, as well as a damn good sniper. Everything matches, same hair color, eye color even. You would have done great if we didn't have all this technology at our disposal. This is one hell of a coincidence meeting again like this, don't you agree?"

"Yes, sir."

"Is that all you have to say to an old warhorse like me?"

"Colonel, not to sound brash, but the last I heard is that you went MIA a few years ago in Afghanistan and now here you sit commanding mercenaries in Canada after North America is almost destroyed by an unknown enemy."

Mark knew that he'd been made and had to roll with it. He knew he couldn't pass up a good thing in order to find the answers to all of his questions, either.

The next few minutes could go good or bad, depending on how he played it.

"Yes, I can see how this all might look. I finally escaped my captivity about five months ago and have been recovering ever since. When we were attacked, I was reactivated and asked to command this, one of many "*Safe Zones*" in North America."

Mark took in all of the *bullshit* this man was shoveling and was very careful about how he proceeded. "Do you need more help, Colonel?"

"I was hoping you would step up, Mark! We need more qualified men like you."

The two men traded stories of times once forgotten and of recent world events while the colonel poured two tumblers of Grand Marnier Cognac over ice and offered Mark a Cuban cigar, which he accepted.

The colonel began by saying, "The terror attack on the western world has collapsed many other countries, too. Worldwide in almost two weeks, millions of people have died, because the instability that followed the bombings here and at home created food shortages that caused riots in most large cities on all continents."

After about an hour, the colonel ended another story and said, "As soon as they told me what your dog tags said and that we had a ghost in our midst, I knew it was you. And I know why you were evading us."

"Why do you think that is?"

"You're a smart man, Mitchell. I would have done the same thing in your shoes. If you don't know your enemy, study them and keep them in the dark until you're ready to strike."

"Well, I for one am glad that we're on the same side," Mark said.

The colonel picked up the phone and said, "Come here."

The small, but muscular man that had brought Mark into the office earlier opened the door and entered the room.

"Sanchez," said the colonel, "take Mark here to the barracks and get him a room so he can get cleaned up. I want fresh uniforms for him and captain bars placed on the collars."

"Yes, sir. Please follow me, sir."

Mark got up, shook hands with the colonel and followed the man named Sanchez. This guy, like many of the others he had encountered so far, was a professional soldier and portrayed a tough-guy demeanor. If it came down to it, he would be a handful, and Mark, in his condition, wasn't ready to find out. He needed to find Andy and Schnell, and figure out what the Colonel's angle was, and why a known extremist was in the so called "*Safe Zone.*"

They walked back to the elevator and went downstairs. It was a short distance to what they called the barracks. It was the old lodging facility for the Olympic Games that had been turned into a hotel.

They entered the room that Sanchez said was Mark's by using a keycard. There were two beds on either side of the room with a flat-screen T.V. mounted on the wall in the center. Mark noticed all of his gear and weapons laid out on the floor with many boxes of ammo for his rifle and handguns.

"Well, that was nice of somebody."

"The colonel wanted you to feel welcome, sir. Your son and canine will be by shortly to join you. A list of activities and times for meals is on your nightstand, as well as an electronic key card that will allow you to enter most areas of the facility, also a PDA that will answer many questions you may have. A man will be by at 0700 tomorrow to familiarize you with our procedures. Will you need anything else, sir?"

"I think I'm good for now."

With that, the man left him alone.

He knew they had gone through all of his belongings with a fine-tooth comb, and may have put bugs in certain items, as well. He would check it all shortly. He didn't see any cameras in the room but knew they were there. They would want to see what he was up to at all times, at least that's what he would have done.

After the man left, Mark grabbed a fresh towel that was lying on the bed and went to the bathroom to shower. A quick shave with the razor on the counter was in order. He trimmed his beard and shaved his head with clippers he found in a drawer, then undressed quickly after turning on the shower. The hot water and soap smell were invigorating once he was inside the stall. Still unsure about all that was afforded him suddenly, he washed and was done within minutes. He looked at the wound on his arm and decided it was healing just fine.

After getting dressed he started sorting through all of his gear when there was a knock at the door. Mark instinctively grabbed his Glock, checked for a round in the chamber and opened the door a crack. Andy and Schnell were standing there with a few men behind them.

"Captain, your son and canine," said a tall, thin black man with a shaved head in an island accent that Mark couldn't place.

"Thank you, Sergeant."

Andy, arm in a sling, and Schnell walked in the room. After the men left Andy immediately started asking questions.

Mark stopped him right away and took him into the bathroom. He turned on the hair-dryer and whispered in his ear.

When he was done, Andy nodded his head that he understood and they went back to casual meaningless conversation.

"What did the medic say?"

"She said you did a great job on my wound but it was a good thing that you brought me here, because it was starting to get infected."

"I'm glad we got here when we did. I think we missed lunch, but dinner should be in a few hours."

Mark continued to look through his gear and get it all in order. He was pleasantly surprised to see that everything was still there, including his gold and silver bars and coins, along with his Cuban cigars. Andy sat on the couch, relaxed and watched some TV. Once he put everything away, Mark grabbed the PDA and started looking through all of the information available. He looked up schematics of the complex and familiarized himself with the layout. He knew his activities would be monitored, so he made sure not to search for anything out of the ordinary.

Sometime later Andy piped up with, "I'm hungry."

"All right," said Mark, putting on the blouse of his new uniform. "Let's go find the mess hall."

Schnell looked at them and whined.

"You have to stay here, girl, but we'll be back shortly."

They left the room and walked down a few corridors before getting to the galley. They both stopped to look around as men in uniforms and what looked like thousands of men, women and children lined up to get food, or were sitting at long folding tables eating. The large room was buzzing with conversation. They both felt a sense of comfort, but at what cost?

"Let's go get some chow, son," Mark said with a half smile.

Chapter Forty-One

Calgary, Safe Zone
Mark, Andy and Schnell

After standing in one of the long lines for some time, they were finally able to fill their trays with lasagna, bread and vegetables. They found a seat after seeing others get up, then ate a hearty meal while taking in the room.

"Isn't this great?" Andy asked with enthusiasm after taking a big drink of chocolate milk.

Mark knew that with the noise level in the room this was a good opportunity to talk to him, so he got closer to the boy and started talking in a quiet voice.

"We came here to get you help, but I think we made a mistake."

"Why do you think that? They patched me up and gave you a job."

"This whole thing stinks to high heaven! I have seen too many signs that this is a bad place. I don't know what's really going on, not yet anyway, but I will soon enough. You and Schnell need to get out of here, and fast. I've found the facilities schematics on the PDA they gave me. You need to leave tonight."

Andy nodded his head showing that he understood. They finished the best meal they had eaten in many days, got up and left the room.

Mark woke Andy at 0200, and they got dressed. He knew that once they started moving around the room at such an odd hour, they wouldn't have much time to get out of Dodge, but they had to do this sooner rather than later. He gave Andy his Beretta and a piece of paper with instructions on it. He grabbed his Glock and they both put the guns in the small of their backs before leaving the room.

Mark moved through the hallways like he belonged there, even though, so far, there wasn't anyone else roaming the area at such an early time of morning. He knew they were being watched on the internal surveillance cameras. Mark needed to find the command center to obtain the location of the extremist Umar Abdul, once he got Andy and Schnell to safety. His PDA only had limited information on it, no list of personnel, so he had to find a mainframe for that.

Rounding yet another corner in the maze of hallways, they came to a common area that neither of them had been to yet.

"According to the map, that door there will lead us outside and to a side exit in the fence."

"Won't there be guards?"

"I'll take care of them if there are."

They opened the door and strolled out of the building toward the gate, which only had one guard in the booth. Once the guard saw them walking toward him, he left his post to investigate.

"You two aren't supposed to be back here," announced the man as he approached them.

"I was asked to check the security on this side of the complex," said Mark, acting official.

"Oh, I'm sorry Captain, I didn't realize who you were," said the young man with a baby face, wearing a baggy uniform. "Isn't it an odd hour to be checking on the perimeter?"

"Our jobs are never done, son. Now show me how secure this area is."

The young man explained as much as he could to Mark, while Andy and Schnell slipped through the gate with Mark's keycard. The guard was preoccupied telling all that he knew and trying to impress the captain, so Mark was able to lift his key card to use inside.

"Hey," he said. "Where did the boy and dog go?"

"I sent them away once you started explaining everything. Are you too tired to man your post and remember things? I can have you relieved right away if that needs to happen."

"No, sir, I'm fine. Maybe just a little tired, but I will try harder, I promise!"

"Carry on, then."

With that, Mark left the area to find the command center. He had an idea of where it might be and headed toward the old Worley Parsons Infrastructure and Environment building near the front of the compound. This was where he had been taken for his interrogation and to meet the colonel.

He encountered a few people walking through the halls, but no one stopped him. He had the uniform and an officer's rank to help him on his mission. He avoided talking, by just nodding his head to anyone he came across.

After checking all the rooms he could access with the card on the first three floors, he headed to the fourth. He entered the elevator and pushed the button. The doors were closing when a hand came through the opening and the doors reopened. Much to Mark's surprise and delight, it was his target. The man smiled at him through his thick black beard. This sent chills down Mark's spine and a rush of adrenaline pulsed through him, causing his cheeks to flush. Abdul hit the first-floor button and Mark hit the roof button. The man glanced over at him with a questioning look and in perfect English asked, "Are you going to the fourth-floor or the roof?"

"I accidentally hit the fourth-floor button before you got on."

The doors closed and they rode up to the next floor. The doors opened and closed, then continued on to the roof. Luckily no one else got on to ride, or Mark would be dealing with them, too. As soon as the doors opened, Abdul moved out of the way. That's when Mark pulled his Glock and made his move.

"Get out now!" Mark commanded as they moved out onto the roof that had a glass dome on top.

"What are you doing?"

"I'm doing what should have been done months, no, years ago, now move!"

The man did as Mark said and walked until he was told to stop.

"That's far enough. I've been waiting for this moment for a long time. Did you really think that you could get away with it?"

"I'm not who you think I am."

"I know *exactly* who you are!"

"Please don't hurt me."

"Are you serious? After a mass genocide, you think that you deserve to live?"

Abdul was about to speak when Mark smacked him in the mouth with the butt of his pistol..

"Shut your mouth, you no-good piece of shit! You deserve to die! I know that once I rid the world of you that another will simply take your place, but *your* atrocities need to be answered for."

Mark spun the man around and kicked the back of his legs, putting him on his knees. He put his handgun in his pants behind his back and put Abdul in a choke hold. The man started struggling and hitting Marks legs before pulling on his arms.

The colonel walked into the courtyard on top of the building, just in time to see Mark snap Umar's neck. Three guards walked out, too, dropping their gear and weapons, then moved in, as Mark pulled his gun. He recognized one of them as the man called Sanchez.

"Do you know what you've just done son?" The Colonel asked.

"I do!" Mark said. "This extremist was wanted on three continents and I believe him to be the mastermind behind the attacks on the western world. The thing that I haven't been able to wrap my head around is why he was *here* in the first place. If you knew he was here and had all of this, as you said, technology at your disposal, then you should have known who he was. And if you did know who he was, was he working for you or you for him?"

"Bravo, Mark," the colonel said, clapping his hands. "Those are all valid questions son. Unfortunately, you won't like the answers, not that it really matters. Who in a position of authority would listen to you? I thought we could use you and your expertise, but you won't stop pushing. You just had to ask the wrong questions and arouse suspicion. You could have been part of the future that so desperately needs to happen. Instead, you get to die with all the rest of the non-believers, but because of your insolence, it *won't* be fast and it *will* be painful."

Mark shook his head as the men closed in on him. His world just got suffocating and small. He could feel it choking him as he put the last piece of the puzzle in place. "He was just the puppet you needed to show the world... *You* are the real face of terror! *You are Umar Abdul.* You *are the leader!*"

Mark pulled the trigger on his Glock while it was pointed at the colonel, but all he heard was *click*.

"Did you really think we would give you live weapons?" he said, laughing. "I had all the firing pins removed for this very reason."

The men that had been closing in put Mark on the defensive. His head was on a swivel as the colonel continued to talk, or pray, actually, in Arabic.

"Glory to Allah, lord of the world, who has created us as Muslims and has delivered us this jihad. Peace be upon those who follow his direct path to the day of judgment."

The men attacked at once. Mark blocked punches and kicks from men who had a variety of talents that he recognized from kung fu to karate, to jiu jitsu, while using his gun as a weapon to help fend off the onslaught.

He expected to die someday, but not here, not like this. He figured his day would come amongst a hail of bullets in some foreign land, against all odds, not on a Canadian rooftop with mercenaries paid to end his journey.

Mark blocked another assault then dropped the magazine from his Glock and threw it at the man moving in from his left flank. As he blocked the object Mark moved over and kicked the man. He doubled over in pain from the blow to his groin. Mark picked him up by his head and *crack*, he dropped limp to the floor. Mark then felt a searing pain in his lower back as a fist hit his left side. The remaining men had produced knives and were now stabbing and slashing.

"Come on!" yelled Mark as he spit up blood from the most recent blow to his face, while holding his lower back where he had just been stabbed.

The onslaught continued as the colonel looked on with a sinister grin on his face.

The man that he saw in the parking lot the day before with the large scar on his face approached him with a stunning aerial display of kicks. Mark moved in hard and fast after locking the slide back on his Glock, and with a quick, upward stroke buried the barrel into the man's throat, crushing his windpipe. He pulled the gun out and blood sprayed with each pump of his heart until he fell down, dropping his knife, which Mark picked up.

"Now there are only two of you," said Mark taunting them. "Come and get me!"

The other two men attacked at the same time. Mark threw his gun at Sanchez while slicing the other mans throat. Mark was cut on his arm in the process and his blouse was turning dark from the wound bleeding. He blocked more kicks and punches, before the man made the mistake that Mark hoped he would. He kicked Sanchez in his right knee, dropping him to the floor. He sliced the man's arm and knocked him down with a knee to the face, then grabbed his arm.

Mark's face was dripping with blood from multiple abrasions and cuts, but he had the man's arm held high and broke his forearm, exposing bone before flipping him over.

"Ahhh," Sanchez screamed in agony, while looking at the compound fracture as blood pumped from the wound.

Mark finished off Sanchez by stomping on his throat and crushing his windpipe. The man flopped around like a flounder until he stopped moving. He gasped for air, his face turned blue, his lips sucked for life that wouldn't find its way to his lungs, and then he quit moving all together.

The colonel raised his Sig Saur 9 mm to Mark's head and said, "Look at me, son."

"I'm not your son, old man!"

Mark turned to look and accept his fate when he saw a flash from a distant guard tower. Seconds later the large bay window exploded behind them and he was splattered with blood as the man that brought the western world to its knees dropped his handgun, stumbled sideways and fell to the floor, dead. Mark grabbed the nearest rifle with a scope and looked through it to see who his savior was. Through his bloodied and blurred vision, he made out Andy holding something in his hand. He zoomed the scope in even more and could see the boy holding up his dog tags, as if to tell him that he hadn't forgotten to give them back.

The good guys had won another battle, and Mark knew that the fight was far from over. But now, what was left of humanity would know that a new day had dawned for the survivors, and that terror had been brought to its knees. Order would once again take the place of anarchy. Life would continue and balance would be restored.

Mark was making his way off of the roof to seek medical attention. Soldiers in camouflaged utilities found their way to the scene and saw the dead men lying about.

"Capt. Mitchell, are you OK?" asked a young man as he approached.

Mark gave him a confused look. "Are you taking me into custody?" he barely managed to say through his swollen mouth.

"Andy told us his story once he left the compound when one of our reconnaissance teams found him. We've been slowly putting the pieces together after the attacks."

"Who are you?"

"We're with the ADF, mate."

"Australia? Why are you here?"

"After the attacks on the United States and Canada, most of the world was sent into chaos. We were tasked with helping our allies. Following the bread crumbs led us here after we entered Afghanistan and learned about Umar Abdul and his plans. The task force you had been attached to and many other people associated with it were all on a kill list. We really didn't expect to find you here. Once Andy told us who you were, we had to make our move on the compound. You can hopefully help finish the puzzle for us. We will need to debrief you once your wounds have been looked at."

Mark was put on a stretcher by a couple of medics and carried downstairs.

The world had changed. Many people had lost their lives, and for what, a cause that only a select few believed in? Would things ever be the same again? Only time would tell. Like many others, Mark had lost so much. Andy was his reason for going on now. They would be a beacon of hope for others to follow. A reason to get up and move forward, to rebuild society.

The real reason for the attacks that crippled the western world was blamed on a coalition of extremist terror organizations. The papers would soon report this to shift the blame from an American sympathizer, someone who had been turned by years of brainwashing by a still-unknown person or persons in the mountains of Afghanistan.

A war was raging on too many fronts to count. The remaining might of the U.S. military along with her allies, was pushing back against the enemy and making headway to retake the states that had been overrun. Only a few countries came to the aid of the west. Others had their own internal battles to fight after the collapse that threatened their way of life. It would take time, blood, sweat and tears, but it would all be worth it in the end.

Special thanks to:

Matthew Cook - For your inspiration and ideas that made this book all possible!

Eric Cox – For your continued support and inspiration throughout this endeavor!

Jenny Neyman - For your detailed editing of my stories.

Joseph Robertia – For your continued support of and suggestions for my writing.

Kurt Kormos - For allowing me to use his German shepherd Borz for the cover picture.

Melanie Noblin – For taking my photos and turning them into art!

Logan Parks – Your photography has been a cornerstone of each book! Thank you.

Sheila June Collins – For your help and support.

Joseph, Kyle, Monica and Colleen for the writing club that we have together and for all the help and insight into the stories.

About The Author

Author Travis Wright was born and raised in a small, Oregon town, where his love of the outdoors first began. He grew up hunting and fishing in the rural Northwest, a lifestyle that transferred easily to a life in the Last Frontier. Wright has lived in Alaska for 24 years and has recently retired from selling guns and is writing full time. He is enjoying a quieter life and has focused all of his time on storytelling for now. He is an NRA-certified instructor and continues to enjoy teaching others gun skill and safety as well as shooting his own guns.

Wright's interest in firearm technology as well as his active duty in the Marine Corps Infantry, are both influential in his work as a writer. While Wright has written poetry off and on for most of his adult life, his work as a novelist began in 2010 with the survival story, "Uncertain Times." Since putting that work to rest, he hasn't stopped writing. Wright's life-long active imagination and curiosity of the unknown have found their outlet in storytelling. The recent introduction of his fifth book, "The Wilderness" is sure to be a favorite.

Wright's current work that started with "DeadHorse" is just the beginning of the "Mark Mitchell Chronicles." He looks forward to many more years of telling good stories, putting smiles on faces and keeping the pages turning.